Outbreak
the zombie apocalypse

Craig Jones

Outbreak

First Edition

Published by E-Volve Books

Copyright ©2012 Craig Jones

Cover illustration copyright © 2011 by Donna
Burgess

Image Courtesy Dreamstime.com

Discover other titles from E-Volve Books at
http://E-volveBooks.com

EPIDEMIC

2

1.

The public didn't take what was going on seriously until the Government cancelled football matches and they stopped filming Eastenders. Yes, the first incidents were on the news but no one thought it was any more than a couple of one off events. It was only when the doors were closed at the Queen Vic and the Merseyside derby was postponed did we start sitting up and paying attention. Since 9/11 we had all become too familiar with the concept of violence, to the point that it kind of didn't hold its meaning anymore. So the news story of the well dressed, clean cut business man who got off a trans-Atlantic flight to Heathrow and then became violent didn't initially have us scouring the internet for bootleg security camera footage. Just another drunk taking the fullest possible advantage of the corporate credit card. I guess some people might even have assumed it was a British politician arriving home from a tax payers' treat. Then a report of a similar outburst in Brighton, in Liverpool and then, getting a little closer to home, in Newport. More details of what was happening emerged; people would feel ill, collapse even, but would lash out at anyone who came to help them. Was it terrorism or some sort of epidemic? Suddenly this was big news, not just on the television but in everyone's in-box.

I thought the first email was a sick joke. It was from a CCTV camera on Church Street in Liverpool. The image was grainy, but good enough so you could make out it was a busy shopping day. On first viewing, all you picked up on was a sudden movement to the left of the screen, but if you rewound it and watched it again, knowing where to look, you would see the woman. She was tall, blonde and elegant. She walked with confidence, her head up, knowing that she was drawing a few admiring glances. Then you saw her slow her pace, stumble and fall face first onto the concrete. For a second afterwards, those around her stop and just look, then some move on and others bend to offer help. There are too many people, you can't see if she is sitting up or even moving. You see one man shake his head, pull out a mobile and suddenly throw himself backward, the phone flying out of his hand, up into the air. If you paused it right there, you saw the blonde woman re-appear for a micro-second, her head bulleting into frame, teeth snapping at the phone, missing, but catching the tip of the man's little finger before a scrum of arms and bodies haul her back to the floor. The man himself falls over backwards, spraying an arc of blood across anyone close by him. The first police officer, strangely in full riot gear, appears at the furthest point the camera covers, and the clip ends.

I watched it three times, wondering how they had made it look so real. Then I started trawling the web for more. The Heathrow incident was right there on Youtube, or at least the start of it was. The camera tracks side to side over an exit door at arrivals. A man in the tailored suit enters the shot from the left, heading towards the door. He is carrying what looks like a leather hold-all and is walking at a pace that will keep him in shot even as the camera continues to pan away to the right. But then, as you watch it, you realise he has stopped and you don't see him until the camera pans left again. It brings him back into focus but he's now down on his knees and another business man sidesteps him, doesn't even give him a second glance. He certainly doesn't offer to help. The camera pans right again, away from the men, then left. The second business man is now also on the floor, gripping his right ankle and shin, pushing himself away with his other leg as the first man, now up on his hands and knees, holds his left hand up in front of his face, fingers spread, jaw moving like he was chewing a huge ball of gum, and then licks what can only be blood from his fingers. Again, the camera view moves. And back again. And now armed police have surrounded him, but his face shows no fear as the clip ends and before I have chance to play it again, the website had pulled it.

I turned on the news channels and started to get used to words like epidemiology and pathogenesis pretty quickly. Whatever this was, it was spreading. It was contagious. It was without doubt dangerous. We were advised to stay indoors, not to travel. We were definitely not to travel alone. We were asked not to panic. No one knew if this was man-made or not. If we lived in a rural area, we were told to stock up on supplies from local sources and sit it out. Don't clog up the roads in case emergency services had to get through. It was all very low key, and if you hadn't seen the footage from the internet, then you believed it. Without bothering to switch the news off, I headed upstairs to wake my brother.

2.

Danny and I had locked down the house and he had then switched on the PlayStation and hadn't stopped gaming since. I had padlocked the gates with two of our motorbike security chains and, as they opened inwards to the courtyard, had parked the black Range Rover across them too, keeping the driver's door accessible in case we had to use it at a moment's notice. The wall that made up our perimeter was solid; the wrought iron gate, painted black with the individual struts about three inches apart, was the only way in or out. The house, just outside the village of Usk in Gwent, had been our family home forever. To say we lived in luxury was an understatement. Dad had patented some bracket that was used in pretty much every car out on the road and we had lived off the royalties ever since.

Ironically our parents had died in a motor accident over three years before, but they had made sure we would never want for anything. We kind of took it to the extreme. Neither of us had worked since; why would we? We had cars, bikes, the house and a regular income. We had our food delivered on a weekly basis and the guy from Tesco had been around the day before all this kicked off. We'd both gone to a private school but I had fared less well in the real world of university. I had lasted about four weeks before I realised I didn't need to be pushing myself through the hard work and dropped out. I suppose I could have had at least made the effort to fail my first year exams but engineering had not been for me. Not when I knew there would always be enough money in the bank account for Danny and I to take life as easy as possible. I kept the garden in order, did most of the cooking and since Danny had turned seventeen we had gotten rid of all the domestic staff that our parent's solicitor had put on retainer. Was that not enough for me to be getting on with? And anyway, was I really a nineteen year old underachiever if I was loaded? Dad had grown up with nothing, so it would have been gratifying for him to know that we would be in a position where we could wait for our lives' calling to come along. Funny thing, it never did. Not that we went looking for it. It turned out that our lack of drive and motivation would keep us safe. We could have been in a city, near one of the outbreaks when it all started, and that would have been it. Instead we were doing what we always did, where we always did it and could sit tight and wait it out.

Except this was the one thing that refused to pass us by, people refused to pass us by. It wasn't even our neighbours. They spent every winter in Portugal, had done ever since Des had retired, putting their dog into long term kennels. But despite us being pretty isolated, people came. Wanting something. Needing help. I guess if there was one thing we had learnt from living this lifestyle was that if you could help someone then you did. Our parents had taught us a few life skills after all. We watched the road, the tree lined route from Usk to

Caerleon, from the upstairs window and when the car stopped at the gates we could see there were kids in the back. What were we meant to do? There was no way that the gates would be getting opened but there was a ladder in the shed. A minute's effort and the family were in with us after they had pulled their Citroen onto the narrow verge opposite the gate, virtually in the trees. I recognised them from the village, Nick and Jenny Williams and their three children; Rob, the eldest at ten years of age, and his two younger sisters, Sally and Jayne. We had the space and the supplies. We had the chance to help and, yes, the thought of our pleased parents played a part. While Nick and Jenny settled in Danny taught the kids how to play his games and they seemed happy.

It had been around midday when the early reports had come in, when I had watched the first glimpses of the escalation of the situation via the internet and it was a little after four when the Williams family had arrived. We had seen and heard cars fleeing Usk all day, idiots blatantly disobeying the advice being offered by the authorities. Surely these were just isolated incidents. There was something going on in Newport but that was far enough away not to affect us here. Lock the doors and settle in, that was the message. With the gates sealed it was a no-brainer; be safe and stay safe.

I was stood outside the front door, just needing some air to alleviate the claustrophobia I was starting to feel with the house being so full. I had enjoyed the quiet for all of two minutes before Nick had joined me. The driveway was about ten square metres, covered in chippings with a double garage, its back wall actually part of the boundary perimeter to the left of the house from where I was stood. The house was old, with five large bedrooms and a whole series of lounges, dining rooms and studies downstairs. It was made out of huge, grey slabs and looked a little like a picture a child would draw of a house, but on a dark and drizzly day. Both Danny and I had en suites and the general bathroom was huge. The Williams family were given the use of the two spare rooms. I turned to face Nick.

'So how come you decided to leave the village? You know, going against the orders and all that? Nothing would make me run. I mean it. Nothing.'

He was short with small, round glasses and although he had lived in Usk for quite some time, he had never fully lost his Liverpool accent which meant he had sharp urgency about him when he told me;

'You haven't seen them. You don't know what you're talking about.'

Nick was interrupted by a rattle from the gate. He looked up and pointed, taking an instinctive step back over the threshold into the house. And he was right, I hadn't seen them but now I had, and all I wanted to do was run.

3.

I couldn't blink. I could feel my eyes drying out but I couldn't take my eyes off him. His left arm gripped one of the metal struts of the gate. His right hung limply at his side, severed at the elbow. It hadn't been cut off, it had been torn away and the ragged flesh of what was left of his bicep was covered in black, congealed blood. A shard of bone poked itself through the mangled mass of flesh.

Surely such a wound should still be bleeding if he was walking around?

The clothing, jeans and a white shirt, were torn in other places, and as my gaze drifted up to his face I saw he had a chunk missing from his neck. His face...

I pulled my eyes from him and turned and vomited on the gravel drive. This was someone I knew. I'd seen him around Usk, at the petrol station, in the shop. He shook the gate, released his grip, took hold and shook once more, unable to understand why it wasn't opening for him. His whole body vibrated with the exertion. Then he looked across the bonnet of the Range Rover and saw us, stretched his mouth wide and let out the noise that surely, right across the country, was chilling people to the bone. It was somewhere between a growl and a moan and it intensified as he began to shake even harder at the gate. While I was hypnotised, Nick fled inside and slammed my own front door in my face. Suddenly, it was the open spaces around me making me feel claustrophobic. I began to panic. I clawed at the door, but still unable to take my eyes off him, off it. The door flew open and I screamed into Danny's face as he pulled me inside.

***

'You've gotta check this out, Bro, seriously.'

Danny had Sky News on. The volume had been pumped up to drown out the wailing of what was left of the man at the gate. The reporter was talking about unprecedented acts of violence breaking out across the whole country. Something about an infection, a virus, that was making normal people aggressive. That if you were bitten, then you became like them. First thoughts were that whatever it was could be spread via saliva. I couldn't take in what was being said, wasn't even hearing the words coming from the television. A state of emergency had been declared. The military had been mobilised and everyone was to stay inside. I looked at Danny. He had a grin on his face that made him look insane. He was inches from hysteria. Nick and Jenny had taken their kids away from the screen which was now showing armed police shooting at an advancing mob. Only some fell, the rest kept walking forward, arms by their sides, making no attempt to protect themselves or avoid the shots. Finally, the police dropped back and the clip ended with a gloved officer shoving the lens of the camera backwards. The studio reporter, a middle aged man with no tie, no makeup and an air of desperation spoke without the usual eloquence of a newscaster;

'And this scene is mirrored all across Britain tonight. Please stay in your homes. Barricade yourselves in. Do not try to reach family or friends. The government has launched counter terrorism measures and will have the situation under control in due course. Once again, it would appear that Britain is in the grip of a protracted and violent attack of some sort. We do not know who or what has caused this, but for now, consider your own safety and we will update you when we can.'

I hit the mute button on the remote and sat on the floor. Danny's grin subsided and he became my baby brother again, the little guy I would always look out for, the person who had been at the forefront of every decision I had made over the last three years.

Had I given up the fun of my teenage years to be there for him?

Maybe.

Would I change a single moment?

Never.

He crumpled down on the floor next to me in front of the television and rested his head on my shoulder. I put my arm around him and pulled him close.

'We'll be okay, buddy. We're safe here. By the time that gate gives out, this will all be over.'

I wasn't sure who I was trying to convince; me or my little brother.

4.

Let's get something straight; the way the movies depict the end of the world is not how it went down. The media kept pumping out the news, so we were constantly aware of what was happening. The internet, water, gas, electricity supplies, they were never in danger of failing. Our telephone was out, but that turned out to be a localised issue and all the mobile phone networks were still giving full coverage. The government had an action plan, a response to the situation and they were implementing their control measures almost immediately. There was a confidence that it was not a question of would we be rescued, it was simply a matter of when. We had plenty to do in order to ensure our minds didn't stray too much to the outside world. Nick and Jenny's three children played games, watched movies and, surprisingly, slept pretty well. Surprising because the noise from outside never abated. Mostly it was moaning, but every now and then it became a more frenzied howl which stopped us all in our tracks. We kept the children upstairs, mainly in Danny's room where he had his multi-media nerve centre set up. His room was at the back of the house so it meant that if the volume was kept up loud enough, they didn't even have to hear the constant cacophony from the front gate.

The internet was awash with rumours, but as ever, the BBC delivered a measured but detailed update on the hour, every hour. We were the only country where this was taking place, and whilst help was arriving from other nations, it was a one way street; Britain had been sealed off from the rest of the world. The World Health Organisation apparently had a bunch of experts in a room in Geneva with a specially designed search engine that picked up on any potential outbreaks from news reports across the planet. According to them, so far we were alone in having to face this. The Global Alert and Response Network were working closely with epidemiologists here to nail the source of the problem and to try to shut it down. It would seem that all of the first cases stemmed from a flight from New York into Heathrow, but that was as much as they were giving us right now. The military had a key role in control and quarantine of those infected. Nick, Jenny and I had ·sat for hours, gleaning as much information as possible while Danny took the role of child's entertainer. He was good at it too, but then Robbie, Sally and Jayne liked most of the same things that he did. He only started paying attention when a special announcement was put out across all channels at the same time. We kept the curtains to the lounge closed. The room was off to the left of the house and therefore the closest to the front gate so we didn't want the children wandering up to the window when they were down here to be greeted by that thing. There were three big, deep, comfortable sofas, none matching, centred on a massive television. Along the left hand wall were book shelves with a wide array of titles from technical manuals to sporting biographies. Halfway along was the now disused open fireplace, blocked up because squirrels and birds would get trapped and die in there, filling the house with a putrid stench. The room had two doors, one leading to the stairs and the other, to the back of the room, leading into the kitchen. Although there was also a dining room and dad's study downstairs with all his historical memorabilia, as well as a loo, this was the room that had always been occupied the most, had always been the centre of the house and full of vibrant life. With the windows covered and the lights off, however, it was a dark and eerie place, with the glare from the television screen casting strange moving shadows upon the walls and floor. In every dark movement, especially on the uneven surface of the bookcases, I saw that hand rise up and shake the bar of the gate. A change on the television screen brought my attention back into the room.

I recognised the newscaster; she was the one who always popped up in the middle of dangerous conflict zones.

'Thanks to ongoing investigations, we are now able to bring you up to date information on the situation engulfing Britain. Do not approach any individual that you suspect has been infected. They will be highly contagious and direct contact must be avoided. The incubation period varies according to the individual but when symptoms occur, they are severe and as of this moment, there is no cure. First, those infected will become faint and may black out. This is followed by what most of us have already witnessed; extreme violence. If a member of your party, whether family or friend, becomes infected, you need to isolate them immediately, even restraining them if possible. There appears to be no other way to stop the infected except to inflict damage to the brain. Help will be with you all soon but you must remain calm, stay inside and ensure the infected cannot gain access. We will keep you updated when we can, but for now, keep safe.'

As if on cue, whatever the person at the gate had become let out a roar. We all jumped.

The screen went black and Danny sprinted out of the room. Jenny made to follow him, but I raised a hand to stop her. I knew him too well; if he was truly upset, he'd want to be left alone. His footsteps thundered up the stairs but within seconds, he was back down again. He had a manic look on his face and an armful of DVD cases and books.

'Zombies', he shouted, and dropped his bounty onto the floor.

Dawn of the Dead, 28 Days Later, novels by Max Brooks and David Wellington. Danny took one of the disks out of its case and fed it into the player.

'I'm telling you, the dead have risen, guys. It's just like in the movies, look.'

He had fast forwarded to a scene where apparently dead bodies sat up from their ambulance gurneys and attacked the medical staff wheeling them out of a block of flats. The police opened fire, but they kept advancing until one of the cops pulled off a head shot and the reanimated corpse, with a spurt of crimson blood, went down for good. Danny hit pause just as the second one was hit in the shoulder and was spun away from the camera.

'See', he said. 'Head shots, blank looks, a desire to eat human flesh.'

I was glad the kids had stayed upstairs.

'Danny, we don't know they eat flesh, for God's sake.'

'Yes we do', said Jenny. 'We saw it happening. We saw our neighbours get bitten. They just…' she trailed off and Nick rushed to her, wrapped his arms around her.

'I don't care what they are', he said, his gaze drifting towards the stairs, clearly thinking of his children. 'I'm just glad we're in here.'

***

Within the hour, Nick's external calm broke. I don't blame him. I would have punched Danny too. Nick and I had been in the lounge, trawling through the channels to find the latest updates. Apparently the Royal family had been in the process of evacuation to a safe venue when the Queen had collapsed. Some reports had said she'd suffered a heart attack and had actually died while others claimed that it was just a sign of stress and she was going to be okay. Turned out it was the former. Jenny called from the top of the stairs, asking if the children were with us. We were both on our feet in a second and were in the hallway by the time she was halfway down from the upper floor. We could hear laughter, which for the shortest time made us all smile and breathe again, until we realised the sound had come from outside. I flung open the front door and took in everything in a split second. There were now about ten of the infected at the gate. They were just stood there, groaning, but hardly moving, just rocking from one foot onto the next. Rob, Sally and Jayne were stood about five feet from the Range Rover, while my genius brother stood on the bonnet with the heavy, decorative sword from our father's study wall in his hands, stabbing at the faces of those the other side of the gate.

'What the hell are you doing?' I shouted as he lined up an eyeball and drove the tip of the sword into the brain of a dark haired woman. He glanced at me as, with a flourish, he whipped it back and she fell, black slime spewing from her eye socket as the groans of those around her intensified. Jenny ran and ushered the kids inside as Danny jumped down off the car.

'I told you, man, they're zombies. I must have nailed six of them and they don't even back off, they...'

Nick punched him. It was a wild haymaker, and with the run up he had taken, it made one heck of a noise as it connected. I swear even the infected

27

stopped moaning for a moment afterwards. The sword clattered to the floor. The creatures returned to their hellish chant.

Nick swivelled on his heels to march back in, 'He's an idiot, a fool, and if he puts my kids in danger again…'

'Yeah, he's an idiot', I agreed, catching him by the shirt sleeve. 'But he's my brother, he's just a kid and if you ever hit him again, you know what side of the wall you'll find yourself on.'

Of course, Nick was right and Danny should never have taken the kids outside, no matter what he had planned, but Nick was a guest on our land and had to know who was in charge here. He nodded.

***

Danny looked up from the floor, his lip bleeding but that moronic grin of his still there.

'Sorry, Bro.'

'You should be, you Muppet, but you need to apologise to them too.'

'I will. Where are they coming from, Bro, and how did they know where to find us?' he asked, turning back towards the gate, wiping the blood from his face.

'I don't…'

I've replayed this moment a million times over in my head. Danny turns, they see the blood, and they surge at the gate. As one. No fear of the sword, no care for the ones in front getting squashed against the bars. Just pure instinctive blood lust. The roar from them made me feel sick to the pit of my stomach. Some were screeching, snapping their teeth together like rabid animals. Others let their head roll from side to side, eyes wide and staring. Even though I knew the gate would hold, I dragged Danny up from his place on the floor and shoved him toward the door.

'See! See! I told you', he smirked, pulling the front door open and stepping backwards over the threshold. 'Fricking zombies.'

I glanced back at the gate just before I slammed the door and had to admit; the little idiot was right.

5.

I ran my hands down my face and shook my head, beads of water flicking across the mirror above the basin in front of me. It had been a long day. Jenny had offered to cook and none of us had felt the urge to argue with her. I leant forward and took a long look at myself. I needed a shave; the sporadic stubble across my cheeks, chin and neck didn't suit me. I needed to sleep; I may not have had dark patches under my eyes but my lids felt heavy and my shoulders were tense. I pushed my hair back with my left hand and held onto the basin with my right, staring at myself.

Was it my imagination or were there more lines around my eyes, deeper crevices along my forehead? And if there were, so what? After what I had seen, after what had gone on just this afternoon, after how the situation was becoming more and more ominous, how could I not have more worry lines? There was plenty in this world to be worrying about right now and everything seemed worse since night had fallen.

***

Nick and I had been watching the zombies from my bedroom window at the front of the house, trying to discern a pattern to their behaviour, when we realised that we could hear a car engine. We looked at each other. Was this rescue? Was this the Army? We held our position and waited as the whine of the car got closer and closer. It was coming from Usk. As it approached, Danny's bedroom door opened and he poked his head out.

'What is it?'

'Not sure', I replied, opening the window and leaning out a little, trying to get a better view of the road. 'Just keep the kids in there, okay?'

'Yeah, of course', he said, agreeable for once, giving a little nod to Nick before he closed the door behind him.

The car was suddenly at our gate and was almost past it before the driver applied the brakes. It slid out of sight and we could only make out the blue roof of the car until the rear passenger door opened and a dark haired woman leapt out.

'You have to help us!' she screamed at the same time as Nick gasped.

'I know her!'

I thought she was shouting up to us. I thought she was in control. But she wasn't. I realised in an instant that they'd seen a group of people, assumed there was safety in numbers and now she was out of the car and running into the mass of zombies.

'No', yelled a voice. 'Get back in the car!'

It was my voice. I could only see the top of her head, saw her turn and look up at the window, saw her continue to move towards the gate and saw one of the creatures reach out an arm and wrap its gory fingers around her wrist. The zombies' wailing increased and they all shuffled towards her and then I think I saw her fall and then there was nothing more of her to see. More of the undead ploughed forwards, and they tripped over each other in their race to get to her, muffling out her dying cries. The passenger of the car got out. He was a big bald guy, tall with broad, thick shoulders and he advanced to help his friend, but before he even reached the back of the car he had stopped, realising that not only was he unable to help her, but that there was no one to help him.

'Get back in the car!' shouted Nick, and as the man looked up over the wall to our vantage point, the driver pressed down on the accelerator and began to move away.

'NO!' the man shouted and Nick let his forehead drop onto the windowsill; he'd seen enough already to know how this was going to end.

As the car struggled to gain traction and snaked along the road, the screeching tyres drowning out the drone of the dead, the bald man must have believed he still had a chance to get inside and threw himself towards the still open door. He missed. I watched as the car disappeared away from the house, the passenger door flapping on its hinges as it sped away. I could not watch as the infected beings at my gate turned their attention from the woman and began to pace towards the downed man, their incessant moaning increasing in both pitch and volume.

I could not watch, but I had to do something.

'I'm on my way', I shouted, shoving my head as far out of the window as I could. The man was pushing himself to his feet and I could see that he had grazed the top of his forehead in his effort to get back into the car. Blood dripped. That explained the added animation of the corpses. Without waiting for Nick and praying that Danny would for once show some common sense I sprinted down the stairs. I nearly lost my balance on the last few steps and slammed into the front door, the solid wood bouncing me back. I opened the door and ran outside, my feet leaving waves of gravel in my wake.

'Keep away from them', I bellowed. 'I'm coming.'

I could hear the bald man's breathing even above the zombies' hungry cries. There was another noise permeating the air; an occasional slap or thud. I had no idea what it could be. I jumped onto the bonnet of the Range Rover and then up onto the roof, keeping my feet back from the gate itself. I leant forward and could see the man, swinging wild punches, trying to keep the zombies away from him. The torn jeans and the huge gash in his left knee explained why he had not run away; he simply couldn't.

'Over here', I called, my voice still seeming to come from outside of my body.

He had clearly had some sort of boxing training and he was managing to pick off the creatures with jabs or hooks as they got close to him. It was also obvious that the monsters were slowly closing in on him and it would not be too long before he was surrounded. He caught my eye and almost grinned as he punched a zombie directly on the jaw, sending it sprawling to the floor with a hoarse croak.

'I can help you over', I shouted, reaching my right arm over the gate, taking a firm grip of the metal with my other hand.

He nodded, blood streaming down across his eyes from his head injury, and began to edge his way towards me, his hurt leg slowing him down but his arms continued to create space in front of him. He stretched his hand towards me and our fingers brushed. One or two more steps and I could at least try to haul him over. Then one of the dead fell forward, pushed by one of its fiendish friends, and it was able to snare his trailing leg. He glanced down and the tenuous contact we had made was terminated as he lost his balance and fell to the floor. He did not even have the chance to scream. I turned my eyes as a man I recognised fell onto him and ripped his nose from his face, blood spurting out, hitting the side of the Range Rover with such force that it sounded like rainfall. I jumped down off the roof and stumbled on the gravel. I looked up at Nick and it seemed like he had not moved; his forehead remained flat on the windowsill.

***

I splashed more water on my face, trying to wash away the memories but they lay deeper than that. I dried myself and walked through to my bedroom. I shook my head as I heard music emitting from Danny's room across the landing. Only he could take this situation and make it another excuse to chill out. Did he have no concept of what was going on outside, or was it simply that his life had left him with no concept of the outside world full stop? I could only imagine how his brain was working, casting himself in the movie of what was going on around us, obviously with himself as the ultra-cool action hero.

As I crossed to his room I cringed inside to see he had his door wide open and feared the worst and that he would be watching one of the movies he had earlier displayed downstairs. I hoped the kids weren't in with him. Nick could do with a few hours without Danny winding him up. Seeing Danny was on his own, I stepped inside and closed the door. He flicked the remote and the screen froze on his wall mounted huge flat screen television, silencing the sound of the music video playing. He had managed to remove every ounce of individuality the original architects had tried to bring to each room in the house. The walls around the T. V. were plastered in movie and gaming posters, a king size bed centred in the room and shelves along the right hand wall, filled with movies, books, a multi-functional sound system, games consoles and C. D. cases. He had a wardrobe on the left of his room, together with a small chest of drawers but his clothes were generally kept all over the bed and floor. The door to his en suite bathroom stood partially open, towels strewn all across the tiles. Under the window, which was positioned opposite the door, sat his computer on a simplistic desk. Every light on each piece of electrical equipment glowed green. Mum would have gone mental. And in the middle of it all, sprawled across his bed, lip swollen and still a little bloody, was Danny. Unbelievably, that moronic grin remained firmly in place. I couldn't help but smile back at him.

'Glad to see you're not overly concerned about the fate of humanity', I said as I crossed the room and perched on his desk.

'Look, we're fine in here. You know it. I know it. Even punchy downstairs knows it.'

'Hey, you've pushed it about as far as I can defend with Nick, so just leave it now. It's bad enough knowing what's outside the wall without having to worry about World War Three inside too.'

'Yeah, yeah, yeah. Look, all I was doing was a little research. If he can't understand that what I found out could save our lives then…'

I'd turned away from him, tuning out his naïve logic and looked out of the window across the river to Usk town proper. The street lights still glowed, of course, but the houses were dark. Something caught my eye, further to the left. I leant in against the glass, trying to catch sight of it again, shutting out Danny's theoretical drivel.

'What… what…what the..? Just for once shut up and look at this. Get over here.'

Danny flipped the remote control onto the bed and came over to the window.

'What are you going on about, there's nothing… What the..?'

I guess he'd seen it. It had used to be the Cardiff Arms pub and it was the tallest building on the main street, just over the bridge into Usk. And someone was in the top room, turning the light on and off.

I rushed over to the light switch and starting rhythmically responding to their signal, assuming that Danny would have the common sense to keep watch to see if our reply had any impact upon the regularity of their flashing. After a few seconds I realised he wasn't even at the window anymore. He was at his computer.

'Danny?'

'This ain't the dark ages, Bro. Well, not yet anyway. I'll find them on Facebook and check out who it is. Go get me the Yellow Pages, the ground floor is a hairdresser's now, I bet it's the staff, and I bet the shop has a Facebook page. Matt, I know you are the older brother here, and to a certain extent 'in charge', but you want to find out what's going on over there, you need to get me the Yellow Pages.'

I did as I was told, digging it out of one of the kitchen drawers, smiling at Jenny and the kids but subtlety signalling with a nod that Nick should follow me. Half way up the stairs I stopped and turned to him.

'Kids okay? You okay with Dan?'

'Yes, mate. The children said he told them to stay well back. What's this about?'

'There are others. Alive, over in town. I think. Dan's about to find out for sure and maybe find a way to communicate with them.'

'Who? Where? Who? How?'

'Let's go find out, but please remember, he's a bigger idiot in front of a computer than he is the rest of time.'

Nick and I flanked Danny as he was sat over his computer, hammering away at the keyboard. There were five of them holed up in the top two floors of the building. Two men and three women. They had barricaded themselves in from the shop upwards and felt that they were pretty safe. They could hear noises below them but as far as they could tell, not even the shop on the ground floor had been broken into. They still had running water but they had no food. They had used the internet to stay in touch with the authorities and people they knew outside of Usk, but we were the first from the town itself. It turned out that Danny had been at the same stage himself.

'And you didn't think to tell us?' I asked him before Nick had a chance to. I gestured with my hand, 'calm down', before our guest exploded in rage.

'There was nothing to tell, Bro. Same info as we were getting off the news. If there was anything different, do you think I would have kept it to myself? And everyone I know locally wasn't on line. With all the cars we saw heading out, I'd assumed everyone had gone. Gone or... you know.'

Yeah, we knew, but saying it out loud made it seem that ounce more real, and after he'd said it I'd wished that he hadn't. The brief silence between us was permeated by the constant wave of hungry groans outside. How the children had blocked it out amazed me.

'They've all been using their personal Facebook accounts to make sure their family and friends are okay and only logged onto the shop one when they saw our lights, hoping we would make the connection. Lucky for them we did, huh? The shop was shut when things turned bad, so they locked it up tight, made sure their broadband was on, grabbed a lap top and sealed every door as they worked their way to the top of the building.'

Danny finger tips flew across the keys, sending and receiving messages in seconds. He had found out that the owner was there, a fat and ironically balding Cockney called Simon we'd all seen around town, his friend John, two of the hairdressers, girls called Claire and Susan and one of the regulars, a middle aged woman called Sheila. Between messages the three of us stared across at the light, at the other survivors in Usk, as if we could see each other.

'Ask them how many of those things are outside the shop' said Nick.

Dan typed.

'They can't see. They're too high up to get a proper view out of the window.'

'They're high enough to open the window and have a look straight down.'

45

'I'll ask, but if they haven't done it yet, they may not want to.'

Across the river we saw the light in the top window of the Cardiff Arms go out for over thirty seconds during which time the computer didn't register any incoming messages. Then it came back on, and the incoming message tone pinged once more.

'Oh, no.'

'What Danny?'

'Seriously. Oh, no.'

Nick and I lowered our eyes from the light in the distance to the message on the monitor in front of Danny. Three simple words. Three terrifying words.

'Hundreds of them.'

6.

'Well one thing is for sure; we can't just sit here
and do nothing', Jenny said the following morning.
Nick had filled her in on the situation in the town
and she had become more animated than at any time
previously.

'Matt? What if it was Danny over there? And
Nick? If it was me? The kids?'

She was right and we knew it. Of course she
was right. But what could we do? We weren't the
ones surrounded by hundreds of those things. Or
were we? When had one of us properly checked
last? Yes, we opened the front door and ensured the
gate was still in tact every twenty minutes or so, but
to actually go out there and count? All the curtains
and blinds to the front of the house were kept shut
so the children would not see anything they didn't
want to see, and that had worked out fine for the
rest of us too. But what it also meant was that there
could well be hundreds of them, thousands even, the

pressure mounting on the gates, the Range Rover slipping inch by inch as they …

… I was surprised to see there were no more than twelve of them outside the gate, plus the six that Danny had put to the sword. Those had been gradually trampled into a red pile of mushy clothes and bones that those still upright paid no attention to. Somewhere out there were also the remains of the two tragic car occupants. The infected just kind of stood there, rocking forward and back in the morning sun as if they had lost the ability of balance and that to stop still would result in them simply falling over. They had become more alert when I had stepped away from the door, for the first time their hands reaching out for me through the bars, but their demeanour had calmed and remained more placid since, even when I had climbed onto the bonnet of the Range Rover. The groaning was the most disturbing part of being this close to them.

A constant, guttural 'MMMMMMMM.'

Some held their top lip in a permanent Elvis sneer, a few opened their gore covered mouths wide, others let their jaws hang slack and loose, but the noise from each of them was identical. Not a single one was looking me in the face, I guessed they saw me as their meat, so their eyes tracked whatever part of me that was moving. To be fair, I wasn't looking into their eyes either. I looked at their blood smeared faces though. Wanting but not wanting to see someone I recognised. If all of these were local people then it would give me some hope. If I couldn't place a single one of them, then they must have come from elsewhere, and that would not be a good sign. Our very first arrival was still there, hand every now and again gripping the bars of the gate and push pulling at it. I knew he was local. A couple of other faces were vaguely recognisable too. At the back, almost going in circles was the short, blonde doctor from town, his glasses still perfectly balanced across the bridge of his nose. And then it struck me. Most of these things were

49

not heavily disfigured. Some were mutilated, yes, like the first one I saw, but the rest? Some looked like they hadn't even been touched. Was it just that the merest contact was all it took? Or could it be that whatever it was that caused this was now airborne?

What was I doing out here? I could already be infected... I needed to get inside. I...

I jumped down off the bonnet and rushed towards the house, my legs feeling weak, jelly-like. I realised I was struggling for breath. I had no choice but to stop and bend over, putting my head between my legs as I inhaled deep lungfuls of air.

What was I panicking for? There had been no mention of airborne infection and most of us had been outside, had been near those things with no ill effects. I had freaked myself out, that was all. I wasn't about to change into one of those things. I straightened up and stood for a few seconds, shaking my head at my own irrational fear.

I broke my own spell and walked onwards, to the front door. I had spotted it, resting just at the bottom of the stairs. I retrieved Dad's sword, now with a thick crust of dried blood at its point. I picked it up, tested its weight in my right hand, turned on my heels and strode back towards the zombies, as they once again stretched their fingers out in a vain attempt to snare me. I stepped to the front of the Range Rover, leaning a little over its wing. From a distance I lined up the one armed monstrosity that had first come to take my normal life away from me. Using both my hands, I fired the tip of the sword forward, just as Danny had done, through the left eyeball and into its brain. His groaning halted immediately. I whipped the sword backwards, expecting a spray of blood, but no more than a dribble ran down his grey, dead cheek

'Die!' He began to fall but was held up by the pressure of the others pushing from the back.

'Die!' He bobbled around, more animated than at anytime previously, and finally fell to my right and out of view.

'Die!' I screamed, throwing the sword across the drive.

I walked back to the house, up the stairs to Danny's room where the three of them, Dan, Jenny and Nick were still discussing helping the five people trapped above the hairdressers. They hadn't even realised I had left.

***

'Twenty. Not hundreds. Twenty! This is totally do-able. What you reckon, Bro?'

They all turned around and looked at me, as if I was meant to know the answer to what they were talking about.

Jenny stepped in and answered for me.

'It is. If what they're now telling us is right, then we can help them. But where've the rest of them gone? Last night there were…'

Nick cut her off. 'I think the key word is night. When are the children most afraid? When can they not get to sleep? But now that the sun has come out, they are flat out across the sofas downstairs because things just can't be frightening in the daylight. And last night when Danny got them to look out of the window, it was pitch black. I'd have seen hundreds. But now? Now it is morning and they are more rational, and they see how many there really are.'

'And if that's all there is, we can get to them. I'm sure of it', Danny's excitement level was almost out of control. 'But the problem is going to be getting out of here. We don't know how many are out there.'

'Twelve', I said, then raised my eyebrows to the ceiling. 'Actually, make that eleven.' The three of them stared at me like I had just become one of those creatures outside. I had some explaining to do.

***

'The key thing is that they don't move very quickly. Everyone we saw get attacked, they ran into them, not the other way around. People were panicking, not thinking. That's what lost them their lives. Not speed, not cooperation. Our mistakes, not their ability to hunt us.'

Jenny was very clear that we could pull off the rescue. Nick sat next to her on Danny's bed, nodding in agreement about every aspect of her description of the enemy. I could not help but think about the man I had watched die. If he hadn't been injured then he would have fought his way clear, that was for sure. More importantly, no one deserved to die like that. As much as I did not want us to take any risks, that was something I didn't want anyone else to have to go through.

Danny had been up all through the night, talking with the five at the hairdressers' on line, convincing them that we could do this. Once he knew the real numbers of creatures waiting just the other side of the bridge in Usk, he was pushing that we rescue them.

Now he had a map of Usk up on his computer monitor, Google Earth and Street View providing more detail than I would have ever thought possible. He and Jenny had talked while Nick and I fed the children breakfast. I felt humbled by how well they were coping with everything. But I guess the fact that it wasn't in their face anymore and that they didn't have to see people that they knew killed or transformed into something terrifying, helped them. They were safe and they knew it. And as Nick had said, as long as the sun was in the sky, they believed nothing could harm them. When we came back up the stairs, my brother and Jenny had their plan fully formed. I had thought we'd done enough by taking in the Williams family, but the more I heard Jenny and Danny talk about getting the others over here, the more I realised it would be so wrong to sit back and just think about ourselves being okay.

7.

Danny crashed past me as I headed up the stairs, desperate for some sleep and hoping that an afternoon nap would re-energise my body in a way that restless nights were currently failing to do.

'Do you know where the binoculars are?' he asked over his shoulder, his training shoes slapping on the steps as he descended.

'What?'

He stopped by the front door.

'The binoculars. There's activity outside and I want to get a closer look?'

'What activity? Over in town?'

He shook his head.

'Then what?'

'Let me find the binoculars and I'll show you. Any idea?'

'Range Rover. Glove box', I replied and he was out of the front door and across the gravel drive before I had chance to tell him to be careful.

It was only when I heard the crunch of his return journey that I realised I had been holding my breath. He closed the front door behind himself and once again made his way past me on the stairs.

'Come on, Bro', he said. 'If you snooze, you lose.'

With Usk being so close across the river it was really easy to forget just how isolated we were out here but apart from Des next door, there were no houses for a couple of miles. By the time I reached Danny's room he had already opened his window and was focussing the binoculars off to the right and away from the town. I edged in next to him. I could see the farmhouse and the attached stables he was looking at. It was probably about five miles from our house. It was one of those places that I probably saw every day and paid no attention to. It was painted white and stood out from the trees and fields that surrounded it. If I thought we were isolated then the farmhouse was a million miles from civilisation. Only one single lane track, about a mile in length, linked the farm to the main road.

'Check out the courtyard, Bro.'

He passed me the binoculars and after a few moments I found the track and followed it up towards the front of the farm. It opened up into a paved driveway, which itself broadened into a courtyard between the house and the stables. I adjusted first the zoom and then the focus dials. I removed the binoculars from my eyes. I placed them back again. I removed them. I looked at my brother. For once he was calm. I looked again out over the fields, across the river, to the farm house. I placed the binoculars back in front of my face and leant forward, resting my elbows on the windowsill.

The courtyard was full of zombies. Men, women, children. They walked and they bumped and they turned and their mouths were open and I could all but hear that sound they made. Some were torn. It was the only way to describe them. Limbs were absent, clothes were ripped, faces were unrecognisable. I began to try to count them but Danny pre-empted me.

'There are at least fifty. Seriously, Bro, I recognise loads of them from Usk. I guess this is where they went after they left the town.'

I scanned the front of house, no longer able to watch the undead and their bizarre dance. None of the windows were broken. The front door looked rock solid. The sun was reflecting off the glass and it was impossible to see inside but if the theory was right, then the farmhouse had people inside and the zombies had been drawn to the scent of their flesh. I placed the binoculars down on the desk and rubbed at my eyes. The magnification was beneficial but the slightest movement made the view jump around like a badly edited movie. I felt like I had a little motion sickness.

'So many of them', I sighed.

'I know, but...' Danny paused. 'If they're out there, then it means they're not in town.'

8.

'We need to keep the gates solid, so there's no way that we can take the Range Rover.'

I felt like I was the only voice of reason in the house, but despite knowing that we had to offer some sort of help to the five people stuck across in town, there was no way I was going to let anything we did jeopardise the haven we had here.

'We won't need to take it; we're going to get them on the bikes. More manoeuvrable, faster off the mark. We'll be in and out before the zombies even turn around.'

Danny had totally bought into the idea. He had trawled the news stations and, in his head at least, had developed a very thorough dossier on the strengths and weaknesses of the creatures outside our wall. He'd found clips of the zombies walking, always slowly, just as Nick and Jenny had claimed. He had footage of them being stopped with fatal head shots, but all we needed to do for proof of that one was step up to the front gate with an ornamental sword in hand. Danny had even found one newscast where a soldier, talking back over his shoulder at the camera as he patrolled an inner city road, had almost walked right into the jaws of one of those things. With no time to aim his weapon, he had simply extended his right arm into a solid jab onto the zombie's jaw. Danny loved the scene. Slowed it down, rewound it, commentating on it like it was a boxing match. The male zombie was taller than the soldier, standing at over six foot. His face was unmarked, his fair hair long and floppy at the front. The white shirt he wore was torn open and speckled with blood. He looked more like someone who had crawled out of a car wreck and was entering the first stages of shock than the walking dead. Except for the eyes, of course. The zombie fell to the floor and the cameraman initially backed off as the soldier had taken up a defensive position with his rifle now aiming at the head of the creature. Then he turned and called for the camera to be brought closer. The cameraman zoomed in over the troop's shoulder. The zombie hadn't been killed, but had been completely knocked out. The sound from the footage was muted but it was clear that there was some debate about holding it as a prisoner or not, and then the soldier shot it, a single bullet in the forehead, and the debate was over. More and more film, more and more reasons why Danny and Jenny felt we could do this with next to no risk.

'But any risk is the difference between life and death. The smallest error and…and… and how are we going to get through the gate anyway?'

'Matt. If this works, you are going to love this.'

***

This time it was Nick who stayed with the children. Danny led me outside while Jenny headed into the kitchen. The numbers of zombies had not increased but that horrible noise intensified a notch as we crossed the driveway. Danny gave them the finger. He didn't say anything, just that grin and a look in his eyes I knew meant no good. The ladder was still leaning against the side of the garage and he picked it up and placed it against the front boundary wall, at the very furthest corner from the gate. As he started to climb the ladder I caught his jeans in my right hand. 'Just be careful, yeah?'

'Bro, this is a walk in the park.'

He got himself to the top of the wall and immediately started shouting at the zombies, swinging his arms around, bouncing along the wall towards them, then edging back to the corner. I mounted the ladder myself, thinking that if he fell I could be up to the top, pull the ladder up and drop it down the other side in seconds, just like when we brought Nick and his family in. I climbed up enough so I could see just over the wall but could also see the gate too. I tried my best not to look at the smear of blood still evident on the road. There was a definite shift in the attention of the monsters, a movement towards the noise Danny was creating.

He had gained their attention, that was for sure, but he was not drawing them away from the gate.

'Danny, this isn't going to work, just get down before you…'

'Have some faith, Bro. Here comes Phase Two.'

Jenny came out of the front door with a half full carrier bag. She kept her eyes on us for the few seconds it took her to cross the drive, handed me the bag and tucked herself into the corner of the wall, where she couldn't see the zombies and, I guess most importantly for her, where she couldn't be seen by them. I looked in the bag. There were two chickens in there. Raw, cut into quarters.

'You are kidding me? This is our food! We don't know how long we are going to have to last on what we've got.'

I knew we had more than enough in the cupboards, freezer and fridge to string this out for a good couple of weeks, but I had to say something.

'Just give me the bag', said Dan, suddenly more sedate now his moment of reckoning had arrived.

'And get yourself up here. You are about to see how we're going to clear the gate.'

I climbed up the rest of the ladder and stood on the side wall, not on the front one with Danny. I could still see the top of the heads of most of the zombies. I told Jenny what to do if both of us fell down the wrong side, but was not entirely convinced she would be able to react at all if such a situation presented itself. There was definitely more agitation amongst the zombies as Danny pulled the first lump of raw meet out of the bag.

'Nice and easy with the first one', he said, and dropped it just off the wall and onto the edge of the road.

The reaction was instantaneous. They moved as one, just as they had when they had seen Dan's blood from his lip and although they were moving at nothing more than a shuffle, seeing that many advance at once was intimidating. I could suddenly understand why people had been caught by these things. As they approached the raw chicken, the groaning grew louder.

'MMMMMMMMMMMMMMMMMMMM.'

They began to jostle each other, those with upper limbs that still worked pushing the weaker ones over into the road or against the wall.

The distance from the gate to the corner where Danny had dropped the meat was about thirty meters. It took the fastest of the zombies nearly forty five seconds to reach it. And when it did, its leg seemed to give way underneath it and it fell, face first, onto the food, slurping and chewing like a crow on road kill. Almost in the same instant, the others lost interest. Some turned and began to walk back towards the gate. Others simply rotated in circles as if unsure what to do next. Danny made that call for them.

'There's more here, you scum,' he yelled, jumping up and down on the spot.

He was now stood directly over them so I leant across and hooked my hand into the belt of his jeans. Realising he was taking too much of a risk he stopped, turned and acknowledged me with a raised palm. He then starting lobbing the chicken pieces further and further away, into the road, and once again the zombies competed in their macabre race. The last chicken leg landed at least five car lengths away from the corner of the wall. As it hit the floor, Danny started counting out loud.

'One... two... three...' and then fell silent, signalling that we should both climb down to where Jenny was waiting.

Danny jogged over to the Range Rover and climbed up onto the roof, clapping his hands and whistling. Jenny retreated to the front door of the house, but didn't go back inside. She obviously wanted to see how this was going to pan out as much as we did. I joined Danny, staying on the ground but positioning myself as I had when I had put the blade through the zombie's eye the previous day so I could track the dead's return. All the while we could hear the sounds they made when they were feeding. This was as close as I wanted to get to that sound. I looked up at my brother and realised that he completely believed in what he was doing. Suddenly one of the zombies was back at the gate, staring up at Danny. I had been miles away and jumped backwards.

Danny laughed, 'Ha, he'd have got you if the gate hadn't been there Bro. But that was about eight and a half minutes, just for them to get back. We can do this Matt.'

I hated to admit it but he was right.

***

'So we can get out. But how do we get back in?'

We were back in the house, sat in the lounge, news channel on with the sound muted. Danny had left the children playing computer games upstairs while we had caught up on the latest updates. The Forces were taking control of the areas immediately around their bases. Did this mean that help might not be far away? The news also told us that the zombies, even the BBC were referring to them by this name now, tended to congregate near to where human survivors were holed up. This explained why they had stuck around at our gate and why they had surrounded the hairdressers' shop and the farm. For what we had planned, this was vital news. Unless there were others humans locked in between the house and town, we shouldn't run into any more groups of those things.

Danny outlined the plan in simple steps..

He made it sound so simple.

'Now the difficult bit.'

It was good to know he did have some perception of the risks involved in what we were really going to be doing.

'If we run into any zombies between here and town, we swing left and head up towards the prison, regroup and try again. If not…'

Danny ran through the crucial stage of his plan. Twice.

Jenny and Nick nodded all the way through. Well, they would, wouldn't they? They got to stay within the walls the whole time.

'As long as we keep those busy', Jenny said, thumbing in the direction of the front of the house, 'then getting back in really is the easiest part. And then you use the same route but in reverse until we've rescued them all.'

'If we wear our full leathers, it'll take more than a glancing blow to draw blood.'

'Okay, but how do they feel about taking such a risk? Have you even asked them?' I hoped this would be the deal breaker.

'Bro, they are going to starve.'

'Then what choice have I got? When are we doing this Danny?'

'If it's dry, first thing tomorrow morning.'

9.

We spent the early part of the evening rooting through the garage and shed to accumulate as many weapons as we could. Danny's nerdiness in front of the television and computer had provided another potential lifesaving gem of information; the zombies, right across the nation, had not yet worked out that glass broke. According to Danny, they had also not realised that animals were food; maybe sheep and cattle didn't smell quite right to them anymore. I wondered whether there had been any horses in the stables across at the farm. But the fact that they didn't even attempt to break in anywhere, even where they knew there were people made us feel that although we were taking a risk by opening the gates, if anything went wrong as long as we could get back inside, then we would be safe. Many of the doors inside had locks on them so there would be a way to barricade ourselves in, and if push came to shove, access to the loft was possible from the pull down ladder in the hatch in the spare bedroom.

The garage didn't offer much bounty in terms of weaponry. A baseball bat that could be cut down for one of us to carry inside our motorbike jacket on our journey into town, a few broom sticks that could be sharpened at one end, a grass rake with pretty strong prongs and an old motorbike chain, one end of which Danny covered in masking tape to create a makeshift grip. We had the sword, of course, and that remained leaning inside the front door, ready for action. Danny and I headed down to the shed while Nick and Jenny spent some time with the children and cooked food for the seven of us. As we walked, I tried to see if Danny was sure we could achieve our goal or if he was simply caught up in the moment.

'We don't know these people, Danny. Is all this worth the risk?'

'Bro, we didn't know Nick or Jenny or the kids until they came knocking. Would you have thrown them out if another hundred zombies had followed them to our front door? No. I know you wouldn't. I've been chatting with Claire and Susan on the internet, and they are just normal people. They're nice and they don't want to die. We can do something about it.'

The shed was, as it always had been, unlocked. It was big, about two metres wide and four metres long, with the door that faced out into the garden. I pulled the door open and stepped inside, right into a face full of cobweb. There was no electricity feed out to the shed but there was enough light in the cold evening for us to see. Due to its size, the frame of the shed was solid and thick rafters ran along both its length and width. Danny reached up and swung on one, exaggerated his grunting as he worked a few chin ups.

'If we decide to throw charcoal bricks and wood kindling at them, then we'll be okay,' I said, pulling a three quarter full sack out of one of the corners. 'No wait, here we go.'

A shovel, some rope, and, most importantly, a hand held wood chopper were behind the bag.

Danny grabbed the axe and started swinging it around, a little too close to me for my liking.

'Take it easy, will you? Come on, let's go show them what we've found.'

'Just one second, Bro', and he was off up the garden and onto the driveway. I realised what he had in mind as I tried to catch up with him and by the time I made it to the drive, he was already on the bonnet of the Range Rover with the axe firmly imbedded in the forehead of a female zombie. Thick, dark blood had spurted across the windscreen of the SUV and Danny was now trying to wrestle the axe head back out of her skull as the lifeless body tried to collapse to the floor. The noise from the remaining zombies changed. The moaning became higher pitched, almost like a cat wailing. Their feet stomped to the ground with more effort, some making slapping sounds as they impacted on the tarmac, others slushing in the remains of the dead. Suddenly the axe came loose, the backwards force Danny had been exerting came into play and the axe pin wheeled through the air back over his head, landing just a few inches short of my feet.

'You idiot. You could have killed me. And what if the body is still blocking the way when we try to ride out of here?'

Nick having a go at Dan was one thing. Big brother putting him in his place was different. He looked like he was going to cry. He didn't say anything, but stood in front of me, head bowed, clearly sorry.

'It's just…' he glanced over his shoulder. 'I hate them, Bro. I want this over.'

'I know.'

I scooped the axe up and laid it against the house wall, then put my right arm around Danny and led him to the front door. 'I know buddy.'

***

Everyone else was in bed, maybe not asleep but behind closed doors anyway. Nick and I headed up the stairs after making one last check on the front gate. The zombies were quieter at night, whether we were outside or not. A few clouds drifted over the bright half-moon and it seemed to have caught the attention of our unwelcome guests. Their heads were all slightly lolling back; a couple definitely had their tongues out.

'Maybe they aren't zombies after all', Nick said as we paused for a moment before going off to our rooms.

'What do you mean?' I asked quizzically.

'Just that thing with the moon, mate? Maybe they're not zombies. I reckon they're werewolves.'

I snorted a burst of laughter, but the amusement disappeared in an instant.

We stared at each other for a couple of seconds.

He forced a smile and went to his family. I closed the door to my room and went immediately into the en suite. After cleaning my teeth I walked across my bedroom to the window, pulling the curtain aside. They hadn't moved, still rocking back and forth. I willed something even more evil to come out of the trees opposite and tear them to pieces. I let the curtain fall back into place and sat on the edge of my bed. I needed to sleep, but once again, I doubted it was going to happen tonight.

10.

I showered and dressed before anyone else was up. I checked out of my window again and the numbers of zombies had not swelled overnight. The rain had held off which meant we were able to go for it. The roads would be dry, so easier to ride the bikes on, and we would still be able to cross the river on foot. I wanted us to check that out for sure before we left, as well as leaving some weapons down by the river bank in case we had to battle our way back to the wall. Next up were Jenny and the children. I was outside on the decking, organising which weapons we would leave for Jenny and Nick and what would be placed at the water's edge. I kind of felt that the longer poles and sticks would be better use to us outside as we would be trying to keep our distance from any surprises and that the shorter stuff would be more practical in any hand to hand combat that may have to take place between the gate and the front door.

Jenny came out onto the decking.

'You're not convinced this is the right thing, are you?' she asked.

'Jenny, I know it is the right thing to do, I just think that the authorities are on the verge of fixing things. The news channels are more positive that the epidemic is now under control and that before long, the zombies will be too. Our Forces are the best after all.'

'You're right, of course, you're right. But they haven't eaten over there', she pointed in the approximate direction of the bridge, 'Whatever they had has long gone, and they could end up doing something stupid when they haven't the means to help themselves. Like the people in that car. How would we all feel then?'

'I know I'll feel a hell of a lot better when we are back in here safe and sound. Don't get me wrong. We're doing this. We're doing it and we're going do it right. I just wish we didn't have to.'

'I think we all wish that we didn't have to face up to any of this, Matt, but we are and we're doing okay. We're doing more than okay here, but those people, they're barely surviving.'

'I know. But we're going to change that, aren't we?'

Nick was the next one down the stairs. He looked like he had managed less sleep than me. His eyes were deep, dark hollows but he did a good job of being upbeat around the children. He was a good Dad. The time was just approaching eight and after having a quick discussion about the weapons that we had, which resulted in us agreeing on how they should be split, I headed upstairs to wake Danny. I could hear noise from his room as I tapped on his door and he called for me to come in. A movie was playing on the television screen and Dan was sat at the computer. By reading over his shoulder I confirmed that he was making the final arrangements with the occupants of the hairdressers.'

'Are they ready to go? They know what to do?'

'Yeah, Bro. We're bringing the girls first, Susan and Claire. They are the quickest and that'll make our life easier for the first run. After we've got them here, we'll go back online to the rest of them, work out any glitches and then go get the rest. Simon says he'll go last.'

'We've got to give the zombies time to regroup in front of the shop too. It's pointless us rolling up if they're still all over the road and we can't get around them.'

'Not a prob. Shall we nip down to the river, then?'

'Yeah let's go.'

We headed down the stairs in silence. When we reached the kitchen, Danny fussed the kids and then went outside to look at what we were going to use as weapons if we got caught on the return leg. He nodded his agreement while twirling one of the sharpened broom sticks, making light sabre noises as he did so.

Nick came out to join us, 'So you guys want me up in Danny's window, shouting directions?'

'Yeah. If you see anything that looks like it is moving just shout the word 'home' as loud as you can. That's the signal for me to get back over the wall.'

'Matt. Bro. I'll go and do this, there's no need.'

'I'm doing this, Danny. Just take that one as read, okay?'

'You still think you're quicker than me?'

'No. I think I'm quieter and there's less chance of the zombies seeing me because I haven't got a huge oversized moon head that reflects my ego.'

'Oh'

'Yes, oh! Now let's do this before I bottle out of the whole thing.'

***

Danny threw a couple of microwave defrosted pork steaks over the heads of the zombies at the gate. They followed the trend we had seen yesterday and turned in pursuit of the raw meat. I was in place on top of the wall at the back of the house, three sharpened poles and one grass rake already dropped over. My eyes were drawn across the fields, towards the farm house. If I could still see dozens of those creatures patrolling around up there it might make me feel more confident that they weren't strolling around the streets of Usk, waiting for us to stumble into the middle of them, but the trees blocked my view. Dan sprinted down the garden and climbed the ladder, pulling it to the top of the wall and dropping it into place for me to descend to the other side. I looked up at Nick who was thoroughly scanning as far as he could see beyond the barrier. He signalled that all was okay with a double thumbs up. Cheesy, yes, but very clear as to its meaning. With him up there and Danny monitoring the corners of the wall, if anything came along, I would know about it.

'Here we go, then', I said and began to climb down.

Upon reaching the bottom of the ladder, I scanned left and right.

Nothing.

I picked up the four weapons and worked my way down towards the river. I expected the ground to be more treacherous but the grass, while uneven, was not littered with branches or anything that may trip me. I reached the trees and turned around. I knew if there was a problem that both Nick and Dan would have started shouting, but I only realised I had been holding my breath after I saw them both showing me two thumbs. The trees weren't particularly dense and picking my way through was not a problem. As I came out the other side I realised what an amazing day it was. The sky was bright blue with a few cotton wool clouds floating by. For the first time I heard the babble of the river as it wound its way over the large stones that made crossing at this point easier. Even without the stones though, the river looked no more than eight inches deep at most. I stared across over the water to the bank on the other side that led to the tennis courts. I could just make out the tops of the floodlights but most importantly, even as I looked up and down the river as far as I could see, there was not a single member of the undead to be seen. The trees blocked out the noise the zombies made and it struck me for the first time that, apart from the river, the world around me was silent. No cars. No dogs barking. No children's voices as they played. Looking up at the sky again, it hit me that there wasn't a single vapour trail left behind by an aeroplane. The country was more isolated than we could have possibly imagined. I laid the weapons against a large tree trunk about five feet from the water and started to head back. I slowly made my way through the trees until I once again had a proper view of Danny and Nick. Both still held out their thumbs and on reaching the open ground I sprinted to the foot of the ladder.

Danny was holding the top of it steady as I climbed.

'Any problems? Did you see any of them out there?'

'Not a one', I replied, reaching the top and helping my brother pull the ladder up after me. We both turned and waved to Nick, who drew himself back inside out of sight and pulled the window shut.

'And you put the weapons against the big log?'

'Yeah. All done.'

But I couldn't help but think we were making a massive error of judgement by not sitting still and seeing this through.

11.

We stood in the kitchen while I took some water on board. I would need to change my t-shirt and I could already smell my own body odour. Jenny had taken the children up to Danny's room and my anxiety levels were starting to grow.

'I want us to double check everything's okay out front', I said. 'Feeding them might have just gotten those things all riled up.'

Dan and Nick reluctantly agreed. I could tell they were just running through the motions to appease me but they also knew that if I pulled out at this stage then the whole rescue mission was out of the window. Danny reached the front door first, and as he pulled it open he turned his head towards us.

'What if we..?'

'Danny! Look out!'

Nick shoved me aside and I fell to the carpet. He wrapped his right arm across Danny's shoulders and bundled him out of the way, both of them bouncing off the banister at the bottom of the stairs as a decomposing hand, its nails long and sharp, swiped the air where Dan's knees had been a micro-second before.

'What the..?

Nick stepped forward and kicked out at the monstrosity that was lying outside our front door. It had no legs and only one arm. In its attempt to snare my brother it had unbalanced itself and now rocked on its back like an overturned turtle struggling in the sun. It was all but naked. Its shirt was ripped open right across its chest, exposing the bloody mess that had once been its shoulder joint. One leg had been torn off at the hip, the other at the knee and it had left a snail's trail of blood as it had dragged itself across the gravel driveway towards our front door.

Apart from a smear of blood across one cheek, its face and head were unharmed and I realised for the first time that it was a woman. Her hair was blonde, short and before all this happened was probably stylish and fashionable. From my position on the floor I was looking right into her eyes as Nick brought his heel down on the side of her head over and over again until a black ooze ran from her nose. Her hand lifted once more, Nick lifted his knee up as high as he could and when he drove it down into her head I heard a sickening crack as her skull split. The hand slumped to the ground.

'Is it dead?' I whispered.

Nick stamped again.

'Now it is', he said and stepped over it onto the drive.

He bent over, resting his hands on his knees as he sucked in air until his lungs were full. Danny followed him out and put an arm across his shoulders.

'That was amazing, dude. Thank you.'

Nick waved a hand dismissively.

'Guys?' I called.

They both turned their eyes towards me.

'Could you maybe drag this thing away from my face?'

Nick pulled himself together and helped Danny to throw the half-zombie over the wall. The undead briefly intensified their groans and made a few investigative shuffles towards the corpse, but then lost interest. We followed the gory mess our vicious visitor had left to the gate and it became clear that its injuries had allowed it to slip through the narrow gap. Logic told us that when the other zombies had left the gate in search of the food then this damaged creature had finally found its way to the front, and into our safety zone. None of us mentioned our concern, our fear, that another one might find its way in.

12.

While Danny and I dressed into our motorbike leathers, Nick rolled our bikes out onto the driveway, placing the customised chain next to Danny's bike and the now shortened baseball bat next to mine. He started the Range Rover and made sure it was warmed up. He also placed the axe on the passenger seat, the handle closest to where Jenny would be sitting so she could quickly pick it up and use it if something went wrong. He set the ladder in the corner of the wall, just as Danny had done when we had tested the zombies' reaction to the raw chickens.

The sword, shovel and the longer kitchen knives were left on the gravel, far enough back so that they wouldn't get in the way of any of the vehicles, but close enough if Nick needed to grab one. By the time Dan and I came out of the front door everything was in place, even the bag half full of uncooked chicken and steaks at the bottom of the ladder. We both collected our helmets, with our gloves stuffed up inside, from the garage and walked across to our bikes in that funny 'I may have soiled myself' way that Kevlar plated leather forced you into. I took Danny's lid while he hopped onto his red Yamaha R6, adjusted the old Adidas rucksack full of meat on his back and started the electric ignition. Danny took both helmets and I mounted my bike, the same model as his but blue and we jammed our makeshift weapons down the front of our leather jackets, zipping them up as far as we could. Jenny came over and pulled them a little more closed. None of us made eye contact and no one was speaking. It was like we were NASA astronauts preparing for lift off. Danny caught my attention and gave me a wink. He passed my helmet to me. At the same time we both pulled our helmets onto our heads, tightening the neck straps. As I got onto my bike and started the engine, Dan dismounted and took up his position at the front of the Range Rover and fished the keys to the two padlocks out of his trouser pocket. Jenny got into the driver's seat of the Range Rover and gunned the engine. She had clearly noticed the now dried, black blood outside the front door and on the drive but I could only guess that she decided that now was not the time to ask questions. She knew I was looking for an excuse not to go through with this and initiating a debate might just have given me the opportunity to talk myself back into the safety of the house. Nick moved across to the foot of the ladder, hooking the bag of meat through his left hand.

It had been decided that I would give the word to get things started. A simple 'go' and Nick would climb the wall and attract the attention of the zombies. I sat on my bike, feeling the vibrations from the throbbing engine in the pit of my stomach. I gave a brief thought to Mum and Dad and the sometimes irritating rule of always having a full tank of fuel that they endorsed to stringently. Well, it was going to save somebody's life now. I realised that until this second I had paid no heed to the zombies at the gate.

Had we become conditioned to the continual groaning?

They continued to rock, forward and back, making that same noise and as time had passed, even just a couple of days, they looked worse, as if they were finally giving in to being dead and that decomposition was starting while they still stood. I watched one for nearly a minute and saw nothing of its humanity left. It was just a shell. I gave the neck strap of my helmet one final tug to make sure it was on tightly enough, pulled on my gloves, turned to Nick and from under my raised visor gave the keyword.

'Go.'

13.

The zombies had reacted to Nick dropping the meat over the wall just as they had the first time Danny had done it. A terrifying version of Pavlov's dogs. The plan could not have been running more smoothly. Danny had quickly unlocked the gates and Jenny had reversed the Range Rover. Dan had quickly pulled the gate open just enough for me to squeeze my bike through and had then got back onto his own machine and followed me out. As we accelerated along the first straight away from the house, I hoped Jenny and Nick had experienced the same lack of problem in getting the gate shut. The roads were deserted. They were also dry and our tyres gripped the asphalt perfectly. We swung around the two tight bends that opened up next to the garden centre on the right and the row of cottages to the left. This was my first point of concern. Where there were homes, there could be people. Where there were people…

Nothing. We rode side by side, straddling the white line as we approached our emergency exit; the left turn that headed up towards the prison. We didn't need to take it. We had every opportunity to go through with this. As we approached town, Danny slowed his bike, pointing for us to divert into the petrol station just before the bridge that would take us into Usk. He pulled in first and I tucked in behind him. When we came to a complete halt, I hopped off my bike and adjusted the straps on his rucksack, making sure they were loose enough for Danny to drop the bag in a split second.

'You ready, Bro?'

'We've come this far', I said. 'Let's get this done.'

I got back on my bike and we rode out of the petrol station, turned right onto the old, stone arched bridge and up onto its apex where we paused once again. From here we could see the rest of the way across the river to the group of zombies outside the hairdressers.' There were twenty at most, probably not even that many, and all were to the right of the road, near the front door of the shop. They had left a clear path along Bridge Street and the rest of the route Danny was going to follow looked entirely clear from our vantage point. The noise of our bikes drew their attention but not enough for them to move towards us. Maybe our leathers restricted the scent of food that we gave off. Just like the ones outside of our gate, they stood there and kind of rocked. I was sure that they were making the same sound too but with my helmet on and the bike's engine purring below me, I couldn't hear anything. Danny flicked his visor up and I edged my bike a touch further forward, so we were once again side by side.

'There's nothing in the way. As soon as we get the signal from them, I'm gone'

'Well, there it is. Good luck'

'You too.'

And, in a blast of sound, he was gone.

A towel was being waved from the very top window of the hairdressers' building. That was our signal that the girls were in place and ready to exit the front doors. All Danny had to do now was draw the zombies away and loop back around. He flew past the creatures, thumb on his horn as he went, trying everything he could to gain their attention. And it worked. They all turned their heads, looking towards the noise he was making and tracked his movement up towards the archway that would take him past the Spar and into the big, open car park. He slowed and swung the bike so he was faced under the arch. I watched with a stomach full of acid as he wrestled with the rucksack, finally freeing it from his back before depositing the mass of raw meat all over the tarmac. And just like they had done back at the house, the zombies reacted and began their shuffle towards the food. I realised with revulsion that there were children in amongst them. A girl, aged about ten with long blonde hair, hair that was streaked with dirt and blood, half her jaw chewed off, stumbled along with the rest of them. And a boy, no older than seven, dressed in a blue and grey tracksuit, dragging himself along behind because he was missing a leg, leaving a trail of gunk behind him like some nightmare slug. Danny waited, knowing he was as much part of the bait as the meat itself. He gunned the throttle on his bike, making as much noise as possible to keep their attention fixed on him as I slowly let my bike creep down the town side of the bridge.

I could see inside the hairdressers.' The faces of two girls, one with short dark hair, and the other with longer blonde hair were now pressed against the glass of the front door, and behind them was a man I vaguely recognised, giving me a wave with one hand and shaking a bunch of keys at me with the other. Yes, they were definitely ready to go.

'No! No! Get back!'

Danny. My attention was drawn back to the main street. To the zombies, still about two hundred yards from my brother. To the now open door of one of the cottages on the left. To the tall woman with short, black hair, sprinting towards Danny. Sprinting into the mass of zombies. Realising her mistake. Trying to turn. Slipping, falling into two of the undead. Screaming as, on her hands and knees, she tried to crawl away from them. Elbows already bloody. A zombie, a bald fat man with its shirt torn open, falling to its own knees and sinking its uncannily white teeth through her jeans into her calf muscle. A spurt of blood arcing up into the air and spraying the nearest creatures. Those that the blood hit stopped and started licking the red liquid off themselves. Her head being thrown back as she yelled for help. A second zombie, falling onto her, ripping at the back of her neck with teeth and fingernails, tearing the flesh, its face becoming a mass of blood and gore. And then her eyes locked on mine. One of her hands reached out for me. She mouthed the words 'Help me.'

The child zombie, the boy who had been crawling behind the rest of them, had finally caught up. Her throat was at the perfect height and he sunk his teeth into her wind pipe, snapping his head backwards, his mouth full of skin and gristle. And then she was engulfed by even more creatures. They squirmed over her wriggling body like a fisherman's box full of maggots. From being so unsteady on their feet, they fed with a frenzy that had frozen both Danny and I to the spot.

Was it because we both knew who she was?

That she was Missus Pound who we saw walking her dog, a friendly golden Labrador, past our house on a regular basis? That she always had time to stop and say hello? That one of the zombies now emerged from the scrum, using others of its kind as crutches as it pushed itself to its feet, with her arm, torn off from the elbow, held like a chicken leg? That her blood was running down its chin and it was taking the time to push the droplets back inside what was left of its lips with fingers that were already caked in dried flesh? Yes, it was because of all of those things. But what got us moving again was when another of the zombies pushed and pulled its way onto its feet, its fingers still wrapped around her hair, with the rest of her head swinging, a section of her spine visible and the last of her blood dripping onto the road. The creature raised its prize up to eye level, confused as to what was weighing its arm down, and simply discarded Missus Pounds' head into the gutter and began walking again towards the fresh meat at Danny's feet. Slowly, most of the others followed suit, leaving three or four of their hellish cohort licking her blood off the white line in the middle of the road.

The roar of Danny's bike brought my focus back onto the task in hand. He popped the front wheel up the curb and was gone through the archway. I advanced across the bridge and turned right, to the front door of the shop and signalled 'wait' with a raised left palm. I could hear Danny's bike in the near distance, still too far away for my liking. I looked back inside the shop and by pointing made it very clear that the dark haired girl was to get on the back of my bike, and that the blonde was to get on the back of Danny's. They nodded their understanding just as I caught the first sight of my brother. He'd made it. He went past me, with a hand raised, and used the junction as his turning circle and also as a chance to check if the zombies were on their way back. He pulled up behind me and shouted, 'We're good to go, they've not started coming back yet.'

I made the universal rolling hand gesture for 'come on' to the girls and after a loud click from the lock, they pulled the door inwards and exited quickly, each jumping onto the pillion seat of our bikes as directed and gripping on tightly. The man with the keys, Simon, just stood in the doorway, staring at us with a moronic smile on his jowly face.

'Lock the door', Danny shouted and pulled forward and around my bike before setting off down the road at a slow and steady pace.

I tucked in behind him, worrying if any cars had blocked our path down Mill Street. But there was nothing to worry about. The road was long and straight so Danny accelerated, keeping to the middle of the street. In seconds we were turning right into the car park. The lush grass of the cricket pitch was in front of us but we turned towards the tennis courts and pulled up at the furthest extreme of the tarmac car park, taking a big loop before stopping so the bikes were facing back towards the exit. Before turning off the engines, we scanned around us for any signs of movement, and, seeing that there wasn't any, we each pushed the red button that cut the power, withdrew the key and stashed it in a deep pocket. The girls got off the bikes and clung to each other. They were understandably terrified.

'Okay, we're heading that way,' I said, pointing towards the bank that led to the river. 'We're going to jog, not sprint. Just stay with us.'

Danny pulled his modified motorbike chain out from inside his jacket and set off, leading the way. The girls went next and I brought up the rear, having paused for a second to extract the cut off bat.

I jogged backwards, making sure there was no reason to turn this into a race to the river. All was clear and I knew we were going to make it back.

***

'Okay', whispered Danny through his visor as we crouched low at the river's edge. 'Head straight over towards that log. We've stashed weapons there. And then head for the grey wall, just off to the left. Can you see?'

Both of them nodded. Luckily, they were both wearing flat shoes and jeans, or the next part of the rescue could have had the potential to turn into a farce.

'Ready?' asked Dan, and we all nodded.

He went first, slowly picking his steps across the river, using the biggest of the stones to cross on, making a real effort to exaggerate where he was going to step next so the girls would know the way. He needn't have bothered. When it was their turn, they simply flew across, not caring if they stood knee deep in water, as long as they could get to the other side and arm themselves with one of the sharpened poles. I joined them last, surprised by the lack of drama, and noise, that the four of us crossing the river had caused. We edged through the trees, spread out with the girls in the middle and Danny and I on the flanks when Nick's voice, barely more than an audible whisper, started repeating 'Clear, clear, clear.'

'Go, head for the ladder', I said, pointing to the middle of the wall where Nick had already dropped our escape route into place.

He stood on the wall above the ladder, gripping it firmly as first one and then the other girl clambered to the top, dropping the sharpened brush poles at the side of the wall as they went. I pushed Danny in front of me for him to traverse next and finally followed him myself. When I reached the top I tore off my gloves and dragged my helmet off my head, inhaling the fresh clear air in huge gulps.

We'd done it. The first two were safe. Danny and Nick were hugging each other, the two girls doing the same.

'Are you both okay?' I asked as I pulled the ladder back up to the top of the wall, and then carefully swung it down the other side, back into the safety of the garden. I dropped my bat over too, Danny following suit with his chain.

'Yes, yes, thank you', the dark haired one whispered, tears streaming down her face, still grasping the hand of her blonde friend.

'Hey, you're going to be okay now' I said ushering them to the top of the ladder and one by one we made our way down, walking up to the back door of the house, everyone politely introducing themselves despite the bizarre nature of the situation. The dark haired girl was Claire, one of the hairdressers and the blonde, Susan, was one of the trainees. They both looked like they hadn't slept at all through any of this and when Jenny met us on the decking they virtually fell into her arms.

'I'll take the girls upstairs, I'm sure they'll want a bath or a shower. I've got everything ready for you, girls, even got something to drink and some food.'

Danny had also removed his motorbike helmet and we both struggled out of our leather jackets. Our t-shirts were soaked with sweat. It must have been the anxiety, the adrenaline, because we hadn't been away that long and it was far from warm.

'You did it, guys!' Nick said, placing a hand on first Danny's shoulder and then mine.

'We've only done the first part, Nick,' my brother replied, suddenly looking grim. 'I'm going to touch base with Simon or John over there and see what the situation is like.'

He paused again.

'Matt, did you see what they did to that woman? Was there anything we could've…?'

'No. She should've stayed where she was. She was obviously safe.'

'There's more people over there alive?' Nick squawked.

'Yeah. Well, there was. She, Missus Pound, she... she got herself killed. Stupid cow ran straight into them.'

'But there could be more people like that? On their own? Not attracting the attention of those...' Nick jabbed his finger toward the front of the house.

'I don't know, I...'

'Nick's right', Danny exclaimed. 'It's like they say on the news. The zombies group up where there are people, not person. Matt, they saw you on the bridge, but they didn't move towards you. They saw me and the meat, and they came that way. One person, maybe even two, doesn't produce enough, I don't know, zombie friendly pheromones or something. But five people, like over there, seven people like here, and we're like catnip for the undead!'

'So what are you suggesting, Danny?' I asked him.

'That things aren't as bad as we think. That the town isn't wiped out. That maybe eighty, a hundred people have become infected. And maybe that number isn't growing because everybody else either shipped out or is locked up safe and tight.'

'There's one other possibility', said Nick. 'They could just all be dead.'

14.

Having spent a few minutes alone on the decking, I walked back into the kitchen and through to the lounge. My black motorbike boots were still wet from traversing the river but I didn't think that was something of any importance given what was going on. Nick was settling the children on the sofa that directly faced the television. It was turned on with the volume still muted, the reporter's mouth moving up and down but with no words coming out. Jenny was upstairs with Claire and Susan and I could hear the shower running in the main bathroom. Danny, of course, was camped in front of the computer, nailing together the final details of part two of our rescue mission. Nick reached across to the arm of the sofa and picked up the remote control, found the volume buttons and brought the news report to full life.

'... officials have once again categorically denied that there has been any evidence of the dead rising. Although the victims of the epidemic are displaying characteristics synonymous with the typical media portrayal of the 'zombie' it is being proven more and more that their state is a symptom of an infection being transferred from person to person via saliva. Tests on the victims have found an as yet unidentified toxin; this toxin is consistent in all cases and scientists are currently working on establishing exactly what it is and where it came from.'

The newscaster paused; it looked as if she was waiting for the next update to appear on the tele-prompter. She looked less strained than previous reporters and it seemed like wardrobe and make up had spent a little time on her. Maybe things were progressing to a faster conclusion than anyone could have expected just a day or so ago. I realised that not only were Nick and myself fully absorbed in the programme, but so were the children, so much so that we all jumped a little when Danny strode into the room and dumped himself on the sofa nearest to the door, boot zips undone, feet hanging over the arm of the furniture.

'What's the latest?' he asked, and the kids all briefly glared at him, raising their fingers to their lips before either Nick or I had the chance to do so.

'As has been previously stated, there have been no reported outbreaks of this kind in any other country and the British mainland remains cordoned off from the rest of Europe.' The long pause again, and this time she actually leant off screen, clearly holding a conversation with someone.

'However, we can bring you... breaking news? Yes, this story is being confirmed as I speak by several of America's largest news agencies... it is being reported that several bodies have been discovered in an isolated farm to the north of New York State. Although further detail is at this time not available, it has been confirmed that at least one of the bodies found is demonstrating the same pathology as those who have been host to the epidemic in this country. We will bring you more on this story as we receive further information.'

We all looked at each other, open mouthed before she started speaking again.

'And back to our headline story. Portsmouth, Liverpool, Cardiff; just three of the cities that have today been confirmed as being clear of the infection. The British military, with some external support, have eradicated the current threat in over twelve cites and continue to make swift progress. However, the public is urged to remain vigilant and to stay indoors, no matter where you are across the country…'

I muted the television.

'Okay, that's it. We're sitting tight. This is so close to being over…'

I didn't think I had to finish the sentence. It was clear to me that the problem was being taken care of, that one or two more days and Simon, John and Sheila would be rescued by the Army, without us having to put ourselves at risk. There was a flurry of noise at the top of the stairs, and then Jenny, Claire and Susan came down to join us. Jenny had dressed the girls in jogging trousers and sweat shirts that were either Danny's or mine.

'You don't mind, do you?' Jenny asked, pointing back and forth to the girls and their fresh attire as they crossed in front of the television and sat on the final spare sofa against the far wall. We both shook our heads.

'You both okay?' I asked. They both nodded, again forcing back tears.

'Look. We're going to hold off getting the rest of them. The news says that this is near over, we can't...'

'You've got to get them out of there.'

It was Claire, the feisty looking, dark haired girl who spoke.

Despite the raw, red eyes from fear and tears, she held a determination in her face. 'Simon has lost it. He just wants to run for it, but he doesn't know where to go for safety. If you don't go back, he'll get them all killed. He wanted to be the first one out of there when you guys said you were coming. He even threatened his friend with a scissors before it all calmed down.'

'If it hadn't been for you…' Susan, the quieter blonde girl, began, but faltered into ratcheted sobs. 'The others, John and Sheila, they need help too. If that fat, slimy…'

She held off finishing in the manner she wanted to when she realised the children were watching her closely.

'Well, there are two people that deserve your help. Please?'

She trailed off into more sobs and both Jenny and Claire wrapped her up in their arms. I'd remained standing throughout and now looked down at Danny and shrugged.

'Don't think we've got a choice, Bro' he said.

'Doesn't look like it.'

'Well, everything is ready to go. We're bringing Sheila and John back this time', he told the girls, then turned his head back towards mine. 'But Bro?'

'Yeah?'

'If Simon gives me any trouble, I'm dropping him'

15.

The theory that the zombies, or whatever Hell had spewed out, found themselves drawn to groups of people, pockets of food, seemed to be an accurate one. We'd experienced it. The girls had experienced it. The people out at the farm were experiencing it. When we led the girls outside to show them what was at our gate, the creatures were as animated as any of us had witnessed. Still rocking back and forth, but with more of a buzz about them, and when the five of us were clear of the front door there was a definite movement from them towards us. Danny and I had already put our leathers back on in preparation for our next pick up. We each carried our helmets with gloves stuffed down inside and our weapons for any hand to hand combat were shoved down the front of our jackets. Danny, rucksack with the last of our beef burgers already in place on his back, was full of bravado, clearly flirting with Susan and to be honest, I got the feeling she was enjoying the attention as much as he loved dishing it out. I guess any semblance of normality at this stage was a welcome interlude for any of us. Jenny was already up in Danny's bedroom window to give us the all clear and Nick had a plastic bag with some raw meat ready to lob over the wall.

'When we get back', Danny said to the blonde girl casually, 'I'll show you how we take care of these things, if you know what I mean.'

'You mean you've actually, you know, killed some of them?'

'Oh yeah. Now we don't need to use the gate again, I'll be finishing this lot off this evening. Send them back to where they came from.'

'Danny, we can't risk blocking the exit in case we need to use the Range Rover to get out of here', I didn't want to belittle him, but I felt we still needed to hold onto some sensibilities. I saw him roll his eyes at Susan, and she barely suppressed a smile, but I let it ride. Like I said, any normality now was good.

The zombies suddenly became even more agitated when Nick pulled the chicken legs from out of the bag.

'You both ready?' he asked, and the pair of us nodded and started to head down the path to the left of the house, towards the ladder that was already in place. As we walked, quickening our pace with every step, we could hear the food hitting the floor after Nick had thrown it over the zombies' heads, and then the louder moaning as they jostled for lunch.

'Nothing stupid, okay Bro', he told me as we reached the foot of the ladder.

'Me? If you can stop thinking about hairdressers for five minutes...'

'Come on! It's a two way street.'

'Yeah, sure it is. She's old enough to be your, well, your older sister at least. Just remember, use the main road around the square this time. I know the telly says they don't make decisions but if just one of them hung around the alley, you'll be trapped.'

He tapped the chain inside his jacket and it made a dampened rattle.

'Not with my zombie killer I won't.'

'Just stick to the plan, please', I implored.

He was halfway up the ladder, turned and looked back at me with that grin.

'Not a worry.'

I followed him to the top of the ladder and turned to the house. Jenny was in the window, both thumbs up to show us the area the other side of the wall was clear. I turned and chose my path along the grass and through the trees. I spotted the long wooden stakes on the ground, pointed them to Danny and he nodded, understanding that we should replace them on the big log. I looked out over the trees. The sound of the river, a slow steady bubble, could just be heard over the moans of the not quite dead at the front of the house. The sky remained almost clear, nature telling us that no matter what mess we were making of things down here, the sky would always be okay. We placed our bike helmets on the wall and between us lifted the ladder, again checking with Jenny, who was now holding her thumbs down.

'Where?' shouted Danny.

'Wait for Nick', she yelled. 'He needs to bring the ladder back up.'

Already we were making mistakes. We shouldn't be going through with this. We placed the ladder back down and made sure it was steady as Nick appeared, jogging down the garden, skirting around the edge of the pond. Without a word, he clambered up and was quite breathless by the time he made the top.

'I sent the girls inside. I thought two of those things were going to start fighting over the meat. But then they seemed to sniff each other, like animals, and realised they were the same. It was weird.'

'Nick', I began. 'Are you suggesting that the zombies trapping us in here are weird?'

He half shrugged his shoulders, and then helped me pull the ladder up and over the wall. Jenny was now giving us the positive thumbs up signal and she had been joined in the window by Susan. Danny spotted her and gave an exaggerated salute as he began his descent. I threw first his and then my helmet down to him, checked my pocket for my bike key, withdrew it and waved it at Danny. He pretended to search his clothing, faking panic, and then opened his left palm to show he had already thought ahead. I climbed down to join my brother and pushed while Nick pulled the ladder back to the top. Danny scooped up the poles, I grabbed the helmets that he had placed on the floor and we set off through the tress to the edge of the river. He laid the weapons in the same place as I had done earlier this morning as I surveyed the opposite river bank. There was no movement except for the running water. Suddenly the air was filled with a giant rushing sound, coming from our right and before we knew it a fighter jet zipped past overhead, following the river upstream, about thirty metres above our head. Danny and I were both rocked on our heels; we must have resembled zombies for a couple of seconds. I wondered for a moment if Nick had fallen off the wall.

'Jesus Christ.'

'Not quite', said Dan, taking his bike helmet from me. 'But it looks like the military are cracking on. Let's do the same.'

We stepped carefully across the river, using the large stones as much as possible. It wasn't just about keeping the noise levels down; if our boots got too sodden it could make riding our motorbikes with potentially inexperienced pillions all the more risky. I made the other side first, turned and let Danny use my trailing hand to pull himself over the last little jump to the bank, which we then scaled together. The bikes were exactly as we had left them; facing towards the exit of the tennis club car

park and not surrounded by zombies. We sprinted
across, mounted our bikes and plunged the keys into
the ignitions. We didn't start the bikes but first
pulled on and secured our helmets and gloves. I
reached over, as I had done at the garage, and
checked that the rucksack straps were loose enough
for Danny to easily dislodge when he needed to.

'Ready?' I asked.

'Ready.'

We brought our bikes to life. We eased the bikes
away and through the gate, up Mill Street towards
the King's Head pub. At the corner we stopped.
This was where we planned to split up with Danny
going right and around the town square and me
going left. I would pause when I could see the
outside of the hairdressers' from level with the
police station. I wondered briefly whether it would
be worth giving a little knock on their door, but it
was only staffed on a part time basis and I could
only assume that if anyone was in there that they

would have tried to do something by now. We both lifted our visors.

'Be careful, Bro', Danny said softly, the words actually catching a little in his throat.

'You too. If it looks dodgy, just turn back. Keep your finger on the horn and I'll meet you back here. You got that?'

'One hundred per cent', he said and then was gone, his bike purring rather than roaring until he turned at the end of the road and then the noise intensified.

I edged my way forward, leaning out over the front of it as far as I could to check the road ahead to get a better angle to view the doorway of the shop. I didn't want to get too close to the group of zombies. They hadn't moved and still just kind of ambled in circles, bumping each other. They looked worse. Where skin had been torn it had now either fallen off or had decayed. Their lips, noticeable even from the thirty metres or so that I was away from them, had peeled back to show off their teeth.

Some had shed at least the top half of their clothes; they looked far more emaciated than I would have expected. After just a short time they were already wasting away to nothing, ribs and collar bones clearly visible through their pale grey, almost translucent, skin. I sat and watched them, disturbed that there was not a single indication of their humanity still to be seen. They were individual beings with a single, selfish cause; find fresh food.

The intermittent blasting of Danny's engine and bike horn, as well as the barrage of expletives he threw at the zombies drew me back into focus. Almost immediately, the horde began their grim exodus, and I was filled with revulsion when they parted and it was clear they had been walking all over the boy zombie, the one with only one leg. It did not stop him from propelling himself after them, even though his hands and forearms looked like nothing more than bloody stumps, leaving gross and gory smudges in his wake. As the last of them disappeared around the corner, heading towards

Danny and the food, I once again took my bike forward. I could hear Danny's bike as he clearly took the shorter route back towards me, catching up with me just as I swung my Yamaha in a wide circle, bringing it to a halt right outside the shop door, facing the way I had come from. Danny copied my manoeuvre and stopped to my immediate right, halfway towards the centre of the road.

'I told you to go around the square', I snapped.

'Made it, didn't I? They took the bait again. They were at the same point as last time when I got out of there, we've got plenty of time.'

The scene through the glass of the entrance to the shop was not dissimilar to the last time; Simon, eyes wild, sweating profusely, stood behind, keys in hand. This time a tall, slight man with light brown hair and a chubby, middle age woman wearing a thick woollen cardigan, done up right to her neckline, had their faces pressed to the glass. I gestured for Simon to quickly check through the windows of the shop on Bridge Street itself that we were clear to go, which he did too quickly for my liking. He then opened the door and the other man, John, sprinted out and got onto the back of my bike.

'Thank you, thank you,' he blurted until I tapped the front of my helmet with an index finger, indicating that he should shut up.

In the doorway, Simon and Sheila were jostling each other. It was clear Simon's nerves had gone and he wanted out right now. Before I could react, Danny was off his bike and reached over Sheila, planting a gloved hand on Simon's chest, shoving him backwards. The woman had now begun to cry, a noise which turned into a shriek when she realised her cardigan had snagged on the door handle and that she couldn't release herself. Her thick jowls wobbled with every noise she made. Danny tried to free her, but looked clumsy in his thick leather bike gloves. Using both his left hand and his teeth, he dragged his right glove off, leaving it dangle from his lips as he pulled the wool free of the handle. He tapped Sheila gently across the face, silencing her and pointed firmly for her to move towards his bike. Before she had chance to react, Simon launched himself at her, wrapping his fist into her hair before the pair of them toppled over backwards into the shop with a startled yelp. Danny flew in after them and I snapped my side-stand down, dismounted and rushed in. He had already separated them and was now kneeling over Simon's chest.

'You fricking idiot. We'll be back for you next.'

Simon was not to be placated and tried to swing a wide punch at Danny, which my brother easily swatted away with his leather clad elbow and then, almost with a regretful sigh, punched Simon flat on the nose. Blood spilled out immediately and the fat little man began gasping for air through his mouth. I pulled Danny roughly off him and to his feet.

'We need to get out of here', I said, right into his face.

I looked around the shop and crossed to the back of the room where there were four white sinks next to the cashier counter. On a row of hooks there were a number of aprons and a few pristine towels. I plucked one of these and threw it at Simon.

'Clean your face up and we'll be back in less than an hour, if we decide you are worth it', I told him.

He let out a murmur of self pity and remained crumpled on the floor.

I hadn't realised it but John had followed me back in and, thank God, he was now calming Sheila. I walked back to Danny and took his right hand in mine. He had grazed his knuckles and blood was seeping from the wound.

'Is that okay?'

'Yeah, yeah, I'm fine, let's go', he said, striding towards the front door. He paused in the door frame, and looked over his left shoulder into the shop.

'My glove?' he asked, as the little blonde girl stepped into my line of sight, just behind him, and in a single bite, removed the little finger from his right hand.

Danny yelled in surprise and pain, his right arm swinging up into the air, sending a spray of blood across the girl's face. He fell back into the shop. John and Sheila instinctively backed off in silence. I rushed to my brother's side, a sound coming from me that could have been the word 'no.'

It might have been because she was young, it might have been anything, but she was more stable on her feet than the rest of those things seemed, so when Simon, dumbstruck at last, lowered the towel from his nose and she saw the blood, she walked towards him, down the clear divide that we had left in the room, and launched herself at his face. From the noise Simon's head made when it hit the floor with all of her weight on top of him, the sound a water melon might make if dropped from the top of a multi-storey car park, he was either dead or unconscious before she actually started feeding on his face. But feed she did, and the chomping, the gnawing of her small teeth on his skin, flesh and bone was too much to take.

'Get out!' I screamed at John and Sheila, my own voice reverberating inside my helmet. 'Run for the tennis club.'

'But...' John said, finger pointing at the back of the girls head as it now burrowed into Simon's neck, and the ever deepening pool of blood spreading out from his body.

'Just go', Danny bellowed, pushing himself to his feet and freeing the chain from inside his jacket with his left hand.

They peered out of the door and were gone out of sight just as Danny wound up his swing and then brought the chain in a wide arc, making contact with the top of the girl's head. Her skull compacted inwards, but without a pause, she continued to devour Simon. Danny's second swing, more of a backhand this time, ended it, actually took the top of her scalp off, and she collapsed over her final meal. Danny dropped the chain and staggered across the shop, his knees finally buckling just in front of the desk. I undid my chin strap and pulled off my helmet, laid it on the floor and then took Danny's off for him, pushing his back in against the desk so he could sit upright. His face had lost every ounce of its colour, of its life and vibrancy. The capillaries in his eyes looked to have exploded. He held his right hand up in between us. The little finger was completely gone. Blood continued to jump out in little spurts. Between pulses I could see the bone running down the middle, sandwiched by slices of finger muscle.

'Oh, no, Bro', Danny muttered, tears and snot running down his face. 'Oh no, oh no, oh no.'

'It'll be okay, I'll get you back... the Army... here soon. They'll have medicine, they'll...'

I was crying too, because I knew I couldn't take him back. Because I knew what was going to happen.

'Bro, Bro. You can't let me...' with his left hand he pointed at the girl. 'So promise me, you'll end it. You won't let me kill anyone, you won't let me...'

He took in a massive breath, making a horrific sound as he did so, his whole body shuddering, his hands pushing out on the floor at his sides, the right one leaving a streak of blood on the wood. His breathing stopped and his eyes shut tight, as if he was in massive pain, his shoulders and neck muscles tight in his agony. I scrambled away, picking my helmet up by the chin section as I stood to my feet.

And then Danny opened his eyelids and his eyes weren't in there anymore. They were a single mass of grey. No pupil, no iris, just a prehistoric grey. I couldn't stop staring into them, and then he opened his mouth and snarled at me, teeth ending the terrifying, guttural noise with a hungry snap. Lips pulled back in a malevolent grin, he shoved his hands violently down to the floor as he tried to gain purchase and get to his feet. I stepped forward and swung my motorcycle helmet as hard as I could, heard a crack as it made contact with his jaw and then drove the back of his skull into the desk.

I stood in the silence for a couple minutes; the only noise I made was releasing my bike helmet and letting it fall to the floor with a thump, settling immediately. I couldn't take my eyes off him. He was dead. Danny was dead. I had killed my brother. I had been forced to kill my brother. Because that little bitch had bitten him and he'd bled and he was still bleeding and the blood was still pumping out of the place where his little finger used to be. And then I remembered the soldier. The one who had been caught by surprise. The one that had used his fist. To knock it out. Like I had done to Danny. Because if he was still bleeding like that, then he couldn't be dead.

Could he?

And if the Army brought a cure with them, then I could save him, just like I had the others. But if they saw him like this, then they would kill him.

16.

Three minutes later I pulled my helmet back over my head and checked through the windows of the shop to make sure everywhere was clear. I'd already rifled Simon's pockets and found the keys. I grabbed hold of his feet and dragged him and his killer as one out into the street, leaving a wide trail of blood from the puddle in the middle of the room right out to the rear of my motorbike. Both bikes were still running, so first I turned Danny's off and slipped the key into my pocket. I ran back to the door to make sure it was properly locked and secure. I mounted my bike and slowly accelerated away, towards the tennis club car park. I was calm. I had to be. I watched in the rear view mirror of my bike as the zombies rounded the corner, drawn this time not by the presence of people but by the smell of food. I tore my eyes away and concentrated on the road, making sure I reached my destination safely.

When I got there, I could see no sign of John or Sheila. I parked the bike as far towards the river as I could, not bothering to turn it around and as I began to walk for home I saw them emerge from behind the trees. I pointed them in the direction we were going and they fell in behind me without a word. I marched across the river, water splashing high up over my boots, paused briefly to collect one of the sharpened brush handles and continued up to the wall of the house.

Nick had the ladder in place but I did not look at him, could not speak to him as I climbed upwards, ignoring the previous protocol of letting those we had rescued go first. Jenny and girls were up in the window. I was vaguely aware of voices, of questions, but I heard none of them clearly as I threw the wooden stake off the wall and into the garden and jumped off the wall myself. I landed heavily and rolled across the grass. I righted myself, collected the weapon and ran as best I could in my leathers. I struggled to unfasten the straps of my helmet as I went and finally dislodged it as I reached the drive, casting it aside towards the garage. I rammed the sharpened end of the wood into the face of the first zombie I could reach. Not aiming for the eye, just wanting to see if it could be hurt any other way. No, it still rocked there, so I lined up the eye socket and shoved the splintered wood in as hard as I could, fighting to keep it upright so I could destroy its face, rip it to pieces and then there was a distant crack and the head of the zombie next to it simply exploded. Then a second, closer 'crack' and another zombie was obliterated.

And then a voice;

'Sir, step away from the gate.'

I continued to probe at its face, the muscles in my arms and back already heavily fatigued, not understanding what was going on, only understanding what I had to do right now to keep myself sane.

'Sir, for your own safety.'

Crack. Mash. Another zombie fell to the floor.

'This is the British Army. We have the situation under control.'

AFTERMATH

17.

I sat on the sofa facing the television. It wasn't on and its black screen was reflecting light from the lounge window, the curtains having been opened for the first time since all of this had began. I was aware of voices outside, of the sound of vehicles moving slowly around and the constant roar of a high pressure water hose. Everyone had finally left me alone. There had been the tears, the exultations of grief, the hugging, but I was cold to it all. It was all I could do to push the vision of the little blonde girl's teeth severing Danny's finger from my mind. Because each time it snuck back in, more detail was added. Like her triumphant smile as she spied the blood on his knuckles, a grin that became a widening of her jaw, that became…

Nick tapped on the door frame and entered the lounge. He had been outside talking with the Army, explaining why I had been so intent on destroying the zombies at the gate, I guessed. He sat to my right, clearly uncomfortable with what to say for the best.

'I've told them everything you've done', he said, and I flinched, making him pause for a second too long, eyebrows raised quizzically. 'And the guy in charge wants to speak with you. He says he understands if after all that's happened that you want to leave it. But we've all told him what you and Danny did for us. For my family, for those girls, John and Sheila. If it wasn't for you, mate…'

I didn't want this. I just wanted Danny back. I got up off the sofa and moved to the window. The Range Rover had been parked back in the garage and a green jeep was in the centre of the driveway. Parked out on the road was some sort of troop transport as well as an Army ambulance. A few armed soldiers were milling about but my attention was drawn to the two people in bright yellow bio-hazard suits. They were meticulously working through the bodies strewn across the road outside the now open gates. They, using what looked like long tweezers, placed different body parts into different bags and once they had cleared a section, a third person stepped forward with the power hose to blast the blood away.

'Will you talk to him?' Nick had joined me at the window and put an arm around my shoulders. My throat felt dry and tight and itchy. I had hardly spoken since my return to the house; just enough to tell everyone that Danny was gone. That he had, in the last seconds of his humanity, run into the mass of returning zombies to make sure I could escape on my motorbike. All this while the Army dispatched the remaining few creatures from outside of our gate and then had left a squad with us and progressed into town. For a while the sound of helicopters had filled the air as they carried out reconnaissance of the surrounding areas. Every now and then I could overhear Nick, Jenny and the others discussing the latest updates they had picked up on from the soldiers outside. Dozens of residents of the village had been killed, most of them returning to stalk the living. Although some had followed the scent of human flesh beyond the town it was considered that most had stayed around, trying to feast on those of us who had chosen not to flee.

Later, the clean up crew had arrived, the people in the safety suits with the bags and the human litter pickers. This drew everyone's attention and had at least stopped them from telling me how sorry they were, how brave Danny had been, that we were both heroes. The children were completely wrapped up in the operations going on outside and I had said it was okay if they watched from my bedroom window. The troops brought supplies for us, and Jenny and Claire spent their time making endless cups of tea and coffee for them. Jenny especially seemed to have thrown herself into this task and had not spent more than five minutes in my company since I had returned with Sheila and John.

I thought about Nick's request. At the end of the day I had to accept that these people were here to help us and to end the siege.

'Yeah, tell him to come in.'

Nick left and went back out of the front door. I could hear him speaking and then a tall, uniformed man came into the lounge. He was a big guy with a long but crooked nose, hair receding a little. I stood as he entered the room and he shook me by the hand with a certain amount of deference, even though I had to look up just to meet his eyes.

'Good afternoon, Sir. I am Captain Alistair Mitchell. I'd first of all like to say how sorry I am for your loss', he said as dropped his eyes respectfully to the floor. He sighed. 'You have both been incredibly brave but I wish you'd have just stayed here.'

His voice was very deep and cultured, Oxford or Cambridge for sure.

'And I wish you'd got here sooner', I replied sternly.

The tears came hard and I put my hands over my face. I was still wearing my leather trousers and motorcycle boots and I knew that I stank. My t-shirt was soaked through with sweat.

'We're going to have to use your house as our base of operations until we secure the town. It would be preferable if your guests could remain here too.'

I blinked away the tears and nodded. What else could I say? Could I handle being on my own in this house right now anyway?

'We'll complete a full search of the town but if Usk is like the rest of the places we've cleaned up, it'll be easy. They behave like pack animals and group together. That's what's made them so easy to exterminate.'

He was obviously trying to be reassuring that a single zombie wouldn't suddenly emerge from one of the shops or houses in town in a week's time. He was being a good guy and was trying to highlight the positive points.

I'd hardly paid any attention to what he'd said after hearing the news that the town would be thoroughly searched. If they looked…

No. That wouldn't happen. I'd been careful.

'Over the next couple of days, a lot of people are going to want to talk to you. I'll be direct and say that some of these people will be critical that you and your brother left the safety of your house. However, I advise you to cooperate.'

'What caused all this, Captain? What is it that caused my brother to die?'

'I'm sorry, but at this point, I'm not at liberty to say, Sir.'

He nodded and left the room. Nick passed him in the doorway and then came into the lounge.

'You okay? Stupid question. I'm sorry, Matt.'

'I know, thank you. I just…'

'Don't, mate. You can't blame yourself, punish yourself. What you have done for us…' he trailed off into deep breaths. I guess he was worried that if he started crying it would kick me off again.

'Look, Captain Mitchell wants everyone to stay here for a few more days, so can you tell everyone to settle themselves in. But to stay out of Danny's room. People will have to sleep on the sofas. But no one goes in there. Make sure they know that, okay?'

'Of course. And thank you, Matt. Thank you for everything.'

***

It was in fact three days before Captain Mitchell returned to the house to inform us that Usk was now totally clear. It came as no surprise to us as the news was full of more and more towns and cities being declared safe. The zombie infestation was at an end. The time we had together was weird. Everyone was naturally elated that the hell that had been just the other side of our gate had gone away forever but they were also very much aware of the grief I was feeling. I was tired of their sympathies, though, and when I was not watching the television, I sat on the decking alone with my thoughts. I think my guests had decided that I had earned the right to do whatever I liked right now, so nobody interrupted me or expected anything from me. I heard the gates being swung open and a heavy vehicle pull onto the driveway. The sky was a rolling mass of heavy, grey clouds. They looked ready to burst at any second and the air was chilly and damp. Even under my blue hoody my arms were cold. I hadn't felt fully warm ever since I had returned to the house without Danny. Every now and again an involuntary shiver would run along the length of my body. I twisted to loosen my lower back, got to my feet and walked around the side of the house to the driveway, where the two guards that had been left to look after us were saluting Captain Mitchell. He spotted me approaching and dismissed his men, who re-positioned themselves just the other side of the gate.

'Mister Hawkins. Good morning. I am sorry to disturb you but would it be possible to speak to everyone?'

'Yeah, sure', I replied, my disdain for what he represented and the failure I felt they were part of evident in my voice. 'Follow me.'

'Certainly.'

I indicated the front door and we walked side by side towards it. He stopped me just before I opened it.

'We have very good people. People you can talk to. About what happened. If you feel it would be any help.'

'I'm doing okay. I needed help. You weren't here.'

'Fine', he said, stepping in closer to me. 'But a time will come when you will need someone. I've seen it before.'

He handed me a card with a hand written mobile phone number on the back.

I shrugged, opened the door and called for everyone to come into the lounge. I didn't offer Mitchell a seat. Nick was the last to arrive and took his place in the same spot Danny had sat in when he had last been in this room.

'Is this everyone?' asked the Captain.

'No', replied Nick. 'My wife, Jenny, she's going to stay upstairs with the children. They've seen and heard enough.'

'I totally understand, Sir. And some of what I have to say is a little sensitive. You will of course bring her up to speed?'

Nick nodded.

'At this point in time we know that two hundred and seventy two residents of Usk itself have lost their lives. If our figures are correct, that's over ten per cent of the town. From what I have ascertained, Usk is a tight knit community. Someone you know, possibly someone you know well or even a family member, may have perished. Not all of those people were killed because of the epidemic, not all of them became infected. There have been a number of automotive accidents, several domestic incidents and I am sorry to report, a few suicides. A lot of people left, most people locked themselves in basements, in lofts, anywhere that they knew to be a secure and safe hiding place.'

My thoughts returned to Missus Pound. She had surely been safe.

'On a bigger scale, it is estimated that there have been around one million casualties across Wales, Scotland and England. The exact figure will of course be determined over the coming weeks and, together with our international partners, we were able to ensure, completely, that the epidemic did not spread outside of Britain.'

He paused. He must have realised that this was a huge amount of information to take in over such a short period of time.

'Usk and the surrounding areas, as far as Cardiff, Newport, Swansea, have been officially declared safe zones. In fact, there are very few areas left that have not seen the eradication of the infected population. For the record, killing them was our only choice. In the time since the first victims came to our attention, our scientists have found nothing that indicated there is a cure.'

'So what caused this?' Nick shouted as he stood to his feet, his Scouse accent more noticeable than ever before, his hands out in front of him, shaking in their desire for an answer.

'That we do not know yet', he replied, looking uncomfortable.

I sighed loudly, exasperated.

Nick sat down, hands now shaking rather than gesticulating.

Claire spoke next.

'And when can we go home?'

Her family was in Chepstow and she had managed to get in touch with them. They were unharmed. Her mobile phone had been lost somewhere along the way but the house phone had been reinstated the day after the Army had arrived;

its failure had been nothing to do with the zombies but had simply been a local fault that the troops had taken care of.

'Well, that is the reason I am here. You can all go home. From today. We have checked your personal details and nowhere any of you live is in a danger zone, so yes, you can go home. I will be arranging transport for each of you.'

He stepped around the room, briefly shaking hands with everyone.

'Good morning to you all.' He saluted and was gone.

***

Many people came and went over the next two days but not a single one of them raised any questions about why Danny and I had been the only ones who had broken the curfew. I wondered if many people across the country had taken risks for other people and from what I was able to pick up on, it seemed that the answer was not many. I could only assume that Mitchell had put the word out about my attitude towards the military because nobody criticised what we had done to my face. Claire and Susan had left as soon as was humanly possible. To be honest, I didn't even attempt to exchange phone numbers or email addresses with them. I don't think they were particularly bothered. John stayed one more night, as did Nick, Jenny and the children. Sheila actually left without saying goodbye, or thank you, to anyone. It was one of the soldiers who told us that he had transported her home. The children were incredibly well behaved but had a million and one questions for us all. They had hounded the soldiers all day and apparently knew more than any of us did as a result. John was a nice enough guy, but if he thanked me once more, if he said how sorry he was one more time, then I was going to have to evict him. He was from somewhere in Kent and would be leaving at first light the following day as one of the Army vehicles was going in vaguely that direction and could at least take him to a base of operations that could then ferry him home. Nick and Jenny were another story. Jenny was desperate to leave. I guessed she realised that I needed some space from all this, that I was putting on a huge front while everyone was still at the house. Although Nick was waiting for one of the soldiers to drive him over to their house it was obvious he didn't want to leave me that he felt he could help by hanging around. His car was right outside, of course, but the Army were still not allowing any civilian transport on the roads until their search had been one hundred per cent completed.

Nick, after a short conversation with one of the soldiers, anxiously awaited while the trooper radioed across to the town. By the time the troop walked across to us Nick was virtually hopping on the spot.

'I've been given permission to take you across in our jeep and leave Private Hayes here at the house.'

'I'll just go and tell Jenny.'

He ran back in through the front door, the habit of closing it over already learnt in such a short time. I turned my back on the young soldier, not wanting to have to make pointless conversation with him. Nick emerged from the front door.

'I shouldn't be too long. If they'll let me in the house I'll check that everything is okay, that the place is safe and then we'll be pretty much out of your hair. You going to be okay on your own? Are there any family or friends you can call?'

'Yeah, yeah. I just need to, well, you know. Get it straight how I say things. I don't want anyone to think…'

I didn't know what I was trying to say but it had the desired effect on Nick. He realised I was struggling and let the subject drop. He patted my shoulder, and he and the soldier were gone. They disappeared around the right hand side of the wall and I heard a tinny engine start up and pull away from the house towards Usk. The other soldier stepped back into sight, taking up a position directly in the middle of the gateway facing the road. I turned and with a momentary pause at the front door, stepped into my rapidly emptying home.

'Jenny? Jenny?'

She wasn't in the lounge or the kitchen so I advanced up the stairs, still calling. She finally emerged from one of the spare rooms.

'The kids are tired. I think I'll join them for a nap', she said softly, head down.

'No worries. Look. I'm going to make some calls, Talk to some of our old school friends. You know? Make sure everyone's okay. Do you need to call anyone?'

'No, no. We'll be home soon enough. Nick says tonight even. Matt, the kids... I just want them settled.'

'Sure, of course.'

She left me standing on the landing feeling quite alone. I went down to the kitchen, got a glass from the cupboard and filled it with water. I hadn't realised how dry my throat was. My body ached so I swallowed a couple of pain killers. I stood at the sink looking out of the window and across the garden until I lost track of time.

I was feeling a little of the pressure on the back of my neck lift when Nick arrived back. He could not contain the smile on his face as I walked through the house and met him at the foot of the stairs

'It's unbelievable over there. I've seen loads of people I know, neighbours, friends, it's… Oh, mate, I didn't mean to be insensitive.'

'Nick, it's okay. Life has to go on.'

'Yeah well for some of us life's only going on because of you and Danny. Nobody's going to forget that. I bumped into Alex Brown. Do you know him? He lives on Mill Street. He saw you and

Danny bring the girls back. He says it was amazing. He says…'

'How's the house looking?'

'Oh. Oh, sorry. Umm… it's fine. We can go back tomorrow. They're going to reopen the roads at some point in the morning. Look. Matt? There's, there's… nothing to be seen over there. They've cleaned it all up. Come and stay with us or a few days, as long as you like. Don't sit here alone, not with… you know?'

'Thanks, but I need to be alone. I need to let all of this out. I just can't with…'

I was struggling. What excuse could I use now when I just wanted them to leave? The patter of footsteps came from upstairs, little voices that had maybe just picked up on the fact that their Dad was back. That gave me the answer I needed.

'I can't let the kids see me fall to pieces, Nick. You understand that, don't you?'

'Of course I do. I'll just go and tell Jenny about the house.'

'Yeah, yeah. And Nick? You can do me one favour when you do go back into town? Just ask them to respect my privacy for a little while. I don't want to be talking through it again and again. That okay?'

He nodded, looked like he was the one that was going to break down, and then turned and took the stairs two at a time to go to his family. I walked through the lounge and back into the kitchen. I took a seat at the table, my mind awash as I formulated my plan.

***

It was Private Hayes who brought the good news to our door at a little after one the following afternoon. The roads were now officially open and the Williams family could go back to their home. It came as no surprise. The BBC had, every fifteen minutes, launched into the headline that the epidemic was over and that all infected cases were accounted for and had been properly dealt with. They didn't come right out and say it but everyone watching, each and every person who had seen what had taken place across the country knew what that meant; eliminated. Nick had been out to the Citroen and started it up, let it run for a few minutes and then, under the supervision of the soldiers, had turned it around and pulled onto the driveway. The tyres had hardly stopped on the gravel before Jenny had one of the back doors open and was ushering the children onto the back seat. She leant in after them and made sure their seatbelts were firmly fastened as Nick got out and made his way over to me.

'Are you sure you won't come with us?' he asked.

'Nick, just leave it be', Jenny called. 'Matt's told us he wants to be alone for a while.'

'She's right. But thank you', I said and shook him by the hand. 'I just need to be by myself. I need to remember Danny and let myself... You know?'

He turned the handshake into a hug.

'You know where we are, if you need anything. I mean it. Anything. We owe you everything, mate.'

'Nick, you're suffocating him.'

He released me from the hug but held onto my hand.

'Anything.'

I tried a smile and half slapped, half pushed him on the back as he turned to get in the car, tears rolling down his face. Jenny approached me, not looking me in the eye, gave me a brief hug and, before I had chance to say a word, opened the car door and got in, waving her hand in front of her face like she was trying to get a bad smell out from under her nose. The kids were all waving from the back of the car as Nick executed a clumsy five point turn and gently eased the car through the gates. He paused, allowing the children to turn in their seats and wave once more, a gesture I returned, and then they were gone. Private Hayes approached me.

'Sir, I've been told to join the rest of my unit in town.'

I shrugged, feeling my lips imitate the sneer that I had witnessed in so many of the infected and the soldier turned his back on me and walked away. I was back inside the house, the door closed, before I heard his vehicle start up and I stood there until once again there was silence all around me. And then the tears came. For the first time I let myself give in to the grief, the shame, the hatred I was feeling. I fell to my knees, my elbows resting on the stairs, and my body shook as the pain and anguish poured out of me uncontrollably. I don't know how long I was there, but by the time I got back to my feet and walked through to the kitchen, it was dark outside. It would soon be time for me to act.

18.

I poured the last of the cereal into a bowl with the final drop of the milk. It was the first thing I had eaten since the toast Nick had forced down me at breakfast time. I didn't feel hungry but knew I had to put something in my stomach to stop the horrible acidic ache I was feeling there. It was close to two in the morning and, looking out of the kitchen window, the sky was dark with heavy rain clouds. It wouldn't be long before a storm hit, by the looks of it out there. Our black Range Rover was back out in the driveway, but this time it was facing the now open gates. I got up from the table and checked the back door was firmly locked, opened the cupboard, took Simon's keys and pushed them deep into the left pocket of my black combat trousers. I had my motorbike boots and jacket on. Leaving the lights on, I marched through the house and out of the front door, pausing to lock it and check it was secure with a couple of firm shoves. I popped the keys into the right hand pocket of my trousers and withdrew the car key in the same movement. I opened the driver's door of the SUV and boosted myself up into the front seat, slipped the key into the ignition and started the engine. I closed the door and turned on the headlights. I was on autopilot, there could be no doubting that, because my body was reacting and moving more quickly than it should have been given the depth of fear swirling around inside of me. Every action was achieved by ticking off an item on a highly precise check-list. The journey into Usk was a blissful blur. It was only when a car full of teenagers from the town passed me going the other way, windows open, arms waving, music and horn blaring, that I paid a little more attention to what I was doing rather than thinking over what I was going to have to do. I eased out right and pulled across the bridge, turning immediately right again, so the hairdressers' shop was on my left. There were more cars parked a little further on, so I tucked in behind the last one, which meant the boot of the

Range Rover was about five feet from the shop door. I snipped the lights off and halted the engine. I got out and walked away from the shop, towards the King's Head, pressing the little button on the key fob, to make the doors lock and the indicators flash twice along with that little blip-blip sound. Placing the keys in my pocket, I walked for about forty metres to where the path diverted left and followed the pavement through the narrow gap between two houses. I kept my head down as I walked, maintaining a brisk pace. I was acutely aware of the amount of noise that could still be heard around the town even at this time of night. Music, voices talking, plenty of laughter. I stuck to the path as it swung left and past the Spar, towards the archway. This had been the route Danny had taken. I tried to get the thoughts out of my mind as I emerged from the arch onto Bridge Street, turned to the left yet again and walked back towards the bridge itself. Light and music spilled from the pub opposite as two people, a man and woman, came out arm in arm. They turned and shouted their goodnights and then, with a shout and a wave to me, began their walk home in the opposite direction to which I was going. As I came level with the side windows of the hairdressers' I could feel my chest constrict and I forced myself to breath slowly and deeply. It wasn't easy. I turned left for the final time, bringing myself full circle. I could see the Range Rover in front of me as I withdrew Simon's keys from my pocket. I positioned what I was best guessing to be the front door key between my right index finger and thumb and, as casually as possible, paused at the door and somehow, more by luck than judgement, slipped the key straight into the lock. It turned first time and I stepped inside, not even bothering to look around me to see if I had been spotted. I closed the door gently, making as little noise as I could and then crouched low so I would not be able to be seen from outside, pushing the keys into one of the zippered pockets of my jacket.

I waited, as had been my plan, for at least twenty minutes. I just sat there in the dark. If anyone had seen me, then they would either have investigated themselves or would have reported the suspicious behaviour to the police station just down the road. I had made the assumption that there would be some sort of presence in there on a full time basis for the coming weeks or even months, so if they did come to search the abandoned shop, I had my story all ready and straight in my head. I just wanted to be close to where Danny had died, just one last time. Even the most hard faced coppers would have understood that, wouldn't they? I sat with my back to the wooden panelling of the bottom of the door. I knew the Army's plan had been to search every empty premises, and I wondered if they had some sort of skeleton key because, despite the door and its lock still being in one piece, they had definitely been in here; the blood had been cleaned up and there was no sign of Danny's chain or the discarded leather glove. It looked like they had finally done something properly. They had clearly not found anything else untoward or the place would have been sealed up.

Every now and then the walls of the shop would be bathed in car headlights and, if the car was coming into Usk from the bridge, the light would often reflect from the mirrors on the opposite wall and blind me with their brightness. I was glad to temporarily lose my vision; I was continuously staring at the shop's counter and what I knew to be behind there.

Time slipped away and I finally began to crawl forward to the right of the counter. I took a deep breath, could feel the sweat beading up on my forehead, and scooted myself around the other side, so once again I could not be seen from anyone peering in through the door or windows of the shop. My last movement had shifted the plain blue rug that covered the hatch into the cellar. The hairdressers' had, of course, previously been The Cardiff Arms pub, and pubs, particularly in buildings this old, had cellars. It was my initial intention just to drag Danny behind the counter and hope that no one would see him, but when, just as it had now, the rug revealed its secret, I knew that I could do even better than that for my brother.

***

I had found the little loop of bronze metal imbedded into the wood, opened the hatch, dropped onto my stomach to look down and spotted the draw string pull for the lights. A single strip fluorescent lamp had jumped into life bathing the room in a yellow radiance. The steps down to the bare concrete floor were quite steep and two of the four walls had metal and wood shelving units bolted to them. Danny still had his motorbike leathers on and I had replaced his crash helmet over his head, but had put it on him backwards so if he regained consciousness he would not be able to bite me. Using the ties from the hairdressers' aprons I had bound his ankles together as well as securing his wrists behind his back. It made it easier when I lowered him down into the cellar, holding onto him under his armpits until I couldn't stretch any further down.

'Sorry, Danny', I told him as I let him fall the rest of the way, the motorbike helmet protecting his head as it slid across the concrete. His body lay at the bottom of the steps as if he were just asleep. If only that was the case. I quickly descended the narrow, wooden stairs and checked what there was to assist me in the cellar. The shelves held numerous hairdressing supplies; peroxide, shampoo, conditioners, scissors, towels, aprons. I dragged Danny into a sitting position with his back against one of the strong looking metal struts that supported the shelving and, after having taken a dozen or so more ties from the spare aprons, attached him to it as tightly as I could. The final cord went around his neck. I knew I had to do this, but it was this last effort that hurt the most. But do it I did, and then I was back up the stairs, pulling the light off as I went. I closed over the hatch, grabbed a couple of towels and mopped up as much of Danny's blood as I could, lobbing them into the pool of Simon's blood as I prepared to leave. I made sure the rug covered the edges of the cellar entrance perfectly. If I was lucky, the next people in here would not find the way down. If I was unlucky, then I was just trying to save my brother. And there was nothing wrong with that.

***

I peeled the rug back and lifted the hatch as little as I needed to reach down and pop on the overhead lighting. It seemed to burn into my retinas after so long sat in the dark. I squinted and closed the hatch over a little, giving my eyes a chance to re-adjust. Once the bright spots in my vision began to fade, I opened it up again, this time just enough to look down and pick out my brother's form. Danny had not broken free of his bonds. He was still tied to the upright of the shelving unit but was clearly no longer unconscious. The heels of his boots had left black streaks along the floor as he had tried to push himself up and his head, still in the turned around motorbike helmet, jerked back and forth like a chicken waiting for its feed. I crept down the stairs, closing the trapdoor gently with as little noise as possible. It was only when I was in the confined area that I became aware of the continual 'mmmm' coming from beneath the helmet, from Danny. I approached him slowly and reached over the back of his head, lifting the visor and then using the space it left to get a tight grip on the helmet. I whipped it off over his head as quickly as possible, tearing small clumps of his hair out at the same time, but making sure my hand did not pass anywhere near to his mouth. I pulled so hard that I lost my balance, falling backwards and away from Danny, the dust from the floor coating my black trousers. I rolled myself over and we sat facing each other. The sudden brightness had silenced him and he kept his chin in close to his chest, his eyelids partially closed over as if the light was stabbing him with tiny daggers into the grey mess that had once been his eyes. His skin was already pale like the others I had seen, tight across his cheekbones and around his jaw. Then he saw me properly and all his fear of the illumination dissipated and he stared straight at me, body rigid, teeth bared by his grotesquely peeled back lips, occasionally snapping but making that evil, terrifying noise over and over and over.

'MMMMMMMMMMMM.'

Maybe being around the military and listening to the formal news reports on the BBC had gotten to me; my brother was infected, but there was no way that my brother was a zombie. For the second time I smashed a motorcycle helmet into his face and for the second time I was not sure if I had killed him or knocked him out. But then, even from his limp jaw, the occasional and distant noise would escape his mouth. I quickly pulled the helmet back into position over his head. I did not want to see Danny in this way. This was not going to be easy but at least it meant that, this time, I could bring my brother home safely.

I snatched one of the scissors from the shelf above Danny and snipped away all of the ties that held him in place. His upper body slumped forward to the floor. His wrists and ankles remained bound. The wound that had once been his little finger was a red, gory mess. It was no longer bleeding but since he had regained whatever form of consciousness that this was, he had been rubbing his hands on the floor behind him, trying to get some purchase, leaving a gloopy smear of flesh and blood on the floor. I was in no rush so made sure the extra ties I put in place around his knees and elbows were as tight as I could make them. By the time I was ready to lift him back up the stairs, I knew there was no way that he could escape and that I, in turn, was safe. Hooking my arms under his, I was able to work my way backwards up the stairs. I used the top of my head to lift the hatch as I stood up more straight and it fell over with a muffled bang as I finally got him to the top. Luckily it had overbalanced onto the rug, which had bunched up on the other side of the hole from which we emerged, so the sound it made was relatively muted. Now, I moved quickly, pulling Danny over as close to the front door as possible and dumping him down on the floor. I made one final trip into the cellar to hide the remains of the cut up ties right under the bottom shelves and used a clean towel to rub up the blood that Danny's hand injury had left behind. I stashed the towel with the torn up ties, mounted the stairs and turned the light off. I closed over the trap door and once again replaced the rug. Crouching, I advanced to the window on my far left. I raised my head just enough to see the back of the Range Rover. I pulled the key fob from my pocket and clicked it to unlock the doors, making the indicators blink once. It must have been quiet out there because I could hear the clunk of the lock opening even in the shop. I quickly ran to every window, checking for any passers by or any people in the windows of the houses that overlooked my position. Nothing. It was time to do this. I returned to the first window and then slipped my thumb to the button at the very bottom of the fob, pressed and held it. The boot of the Range Rover opened. That was my cue to move quickly. I crossed to Danny and, using my right arm, pulled him to his feet, realising for the first time just how light he felt. I got him balanced between my arm and my right hip, my hand gripping the leather of his jacket as tightly as I could. With my left hand I opened the shop door, let it swing inwards and then bundled Danny towards the boot of my vehicle. From a distance, even with the helmet, it would have looked like I was man-handling a drunk and as long as it seemed like we had just come around the corner as opposed to having exited the hairdressers' maybe this would work. I half carried, half dragged his upright body as quickly as I could to the back of the Range Rover, basically throwing him in. I closed the boot with as much grace as possible, locked the car again and walked back past the shop door, casually reaching in and pulling it towards me as I went. It made a dull but resonant noise of metal on metal as the mechanisms slotted into place. I walked back to the Range Rover, clicked the lock and got in, hoping that no one had seen me but mainly hoping that my brother would not get free.

19.

I unravelled the rope and considered where it should be looped up over the rafters. I had to be sure I was positioning him in the right place. I didn't want him too close to the door, although I didn't want him too far out of sight of the open door either; I needed to know straight away before I even stepped inside the shed if he had gotten himself loose at all. I couldn't position him too close to the side panel either because if he started to kick out, not only could he damage the wood but he might also draw attention to himself. That would not be good.

The rafters overlapped in several places and one junction, just off to the left of the centre of the shed, seemed to present the best option. I threaded the rope over the top, tied it off a couple of times, took the longest end over again, knotted and repeated once more. The two ends of rope left hanging were about three feet long and I swung on them, making sure both the rope and the wood were strong enough. They were. That was good enough for me. It was time to bring Danny down. I had too many keys in my trouser pocket, so I diverted into the kitchen and left the house keys and Simon's hairdresser shop keys on the table. The car keys and the padlock keys remained with me. I had not been sure how I was going to secure the shed door and had searched around the garage over the last couple of days of the Williams' stay and had only found one small and rusted hasp and just enough screws to hold it in place. It had not taken long to screw it into position and one of our bike padlocks would do for the time being until I was able to get two far more substantial security devices.

I pressed the button that opened the boot and leant over my brother to see if he had come round yet. His body was still limp, the helmet still on his head and it was easy to drag him out and down the path. The padlock lay on the floor just outside of the shed and was opened, ready to be snipped into place. I gently lay Danny on the grass next to it and pulled the shed open, wedged it wide with my left foot and with no ceremony at all, virtually bounced Danny inside. I let the door swing shut and stepped fully in after him. I realised that I possibly had not thought this through enough. How was I meant to hold him up and tie his hands at the same time? Some engineer I would have turned out to be. He still made no sound and had not made any voluntary movements, so I lifted him to his feet with my left arm under his left armpit. I raised the arm up and stretched over across his chest with my right hand and wrapped one of the loose strands of rope around his wrist, pushing the sleeve of his leather jacket up his forearm as I did so. Holding onto the rope tightly with my right hand, I slid my left hand up to his arm and grabbed hold of the jacket as hard as I could, stepping back slightly and letting Danny's weight slip off me. He stayed upright, and I had just enough hold on him to stop him from sliding to the floor again. I worked quickly, feeling gravity turn against me but within a couple of minutes, he was tightly tied to the rafter.

I had chosen his left hand intentionally. The thought of touching where the girl had bitten him repulsed me. It was from that point where the infection had spread, had taken over his whole body. Maybe the infection was still spreading? And what if it was emanating from that very source? I undid his leather jacket and tried to take it off him, and only got it halfway down his right arm before realising I would never get it off his bound left wrist. To rectify my mistake, I exited the shed and ran up towards the house to fetch the heavy duty scissors from the cutlery draw. I stopped halfway.

Damn.

I had to get into the right habits from the off, and one of those would be to always keep the shed locked. It may only be for a few seconds, but it was not a risk I was prepared to take, full stop. I jogged back, put the padlock in place and this time walked up to the house. When I approached the back door, the security light blinked on. It did not have time to switch itself off before I was back out again, scissors in hand. I retrieved the keys from my pocket, unlocked the shed and stepped back inside.

Danny was no longer hanging there by his left arm. He must have started to regain his senses and now his feet held him up. Not all his senses had returned, however, as he was still blinded by the motorcycle helmet, and I was glad of that when his right arm started trying to grab the air around him, restricted by still being half stuck in the sleeve of the jacket. I was able to pivot away from it but realised I would need to get more rope.

What if he managed to free himself before then? And what about the infection spreading even further?

I looked at the exposed flesh of his upper right arm, just below his shoulder. I looked at the place where his little finger should be, the rest of the digits still wiggling slowly next to the bloody stump. I looked at the small axe, the hatchet, and I knew what I had to do. I picked it up and stepped to Danny's left so I was stood safely behind him. I lined up my swing in the narrow space between his body and the wooden panel and then I sunk the head of the weapon into his arm, just where the bottom of the deltoid shoulder muscle met his bicep. The flesh and muscle tore open, and a little black gooey blood seeped out. There had been a splintering sound of bone breaking on contact and I now had to work the axe up and down to free it from the arm. I could see my own reflection in the motorcycle helmet and I scared myself. If Danny felt any pain, he did not show it; the only time he showed any awareness of what I was doing was when he turned his head towards the wound, as if he felt nothing more than some minor irritation like an insect had landed on him. I swung once more, this time almost going all the way through. Three more swipes at it, and my brother's right arm fell to the floor, leaving a messy, ragged stump that continued to probe the air, searching for food. I kicked the arm into the far corner and ran outside, sick spilling from the sides of my closed mouth as I tried to hold it in.

I had disfigured my brother. Was there anything worse I could do to him? I stepped back inside, my legs shaking, my chest crushing my lungs so breathing hurt. I cut the leather jacket off his arm with the scissors then removed it from him completely so that he was left hanging in his boots, leather trousers and a filthy white t-shirt. The gore had soaked up from his right shoulder along the material. He occasionally tugged on the rope that held him but made little effort to really pull himself free. His feet hardly moved and just shuffled an inch or so forward and back when he lost his balance slightly. I stood behind him, gripped the sides of the helmet with both hands and gently eased it off his head. Either I had gotten used to the noise already or he had not been making it while his face was covered, but the sudden 'MMMM' sound made me drop the helmet. That made up my mind for me. When I wasn't down here with him, talking to him, feeding him, then the helmet would stay on. Leaving it where it lay for now, I stepped around to the front of my brother. His face was almost the same colour grey as his eyes. His hair seemed to be falling out and his lips were pulled back, revealing his out of place white teeth. His gums were bleeding and his tongue licked and flicked around inside his mouth, relishing the taste. I guessed they all did that, sucking their teeth clean as they sought every morsel of food possible. His eyes picked up my movement, as if he had initially been looking through a haze, and he sniffed quickly, fox-like, before launching himself at me, face first. I was well out of his reach, thank God, because the power with which his jaws smashed together caused one of his teeth to chip, the white enamel skating across the shed floor. He started making the growling noise again. His jaw continued to work itself up and down, extending out towards me with every bite. I knew that I had to do something to minimise the risk to myself. I was all too aware that Danny would need feeding, but there was no way in the world that I could manage it if every time I brought him fresh meat he was more interested in chewing on me instead. No, I had to make this as practical for me as possible.

I picked up the shovel, raised it to head height and gently eased the bottom of the blade into Danny's mouth, pressing down so his teeth parted as wide as they would go. Stepping in a little closer, I maintained the downward pressure but also pushed the handle of the shovel up and away from me, using the front of Danny's face as a fulcrum. Even with me being so close, Danny had no instinct to back off despite what was being done to his mouth. I was food and if he could get closer to me, then he could feed, so he pressed forward making my job massively simpler. As the rapidly wasting ligaments in his jaw gave way, first one and then the other side of the mandible popped out of position and when I withdrew the shovel, the lower half of his face was slack and sagging. I stepped back and placed the shovel against the side wall, watching Danny as he tried to bring his teeth together with no success. I realised that Danny was not making any noise. I looked at him and sighed deeply.

What in God's name was I doing?

I couldn't be sure that the further injury I had inflicted upon him by dislocating his jaw was actually going to keep him quiet permanently, so I replaced the motorbike helmet. He didn't resist me. Was he getting used to this way of existing already? I picked up the shovel once more, exited the shed and locked the door quickly. I then wedged the shovel between the door and the floor but I was fairly certain that Danny had neither the ability nor inclination to free himself from his prison. Once the morning came my plan was to either go to the shop and get food for the two of us or to check if the Tesco delivery service was back on track yet. I left the Range Rover where it was but walked to the front of the house and closed the gates over. Even though I didn't have to anymore, it was a habit I was going to find tough to break. I rounded the house and entered the kitchen via the back door. The lights still burnt. My mobile phone was on the table and had been on silent all night. I picked it up and checked the missed calls. There were seven from Nick alone. I would return the calls tomorrow. For now I had to think; I had got him back here but how could I make sure no one found him?

20.

I had lost all track of time. I often did when I was sat with Danny. He stood there, his left arm, of course, still tied tightly to the rafter. The door to the shed was pulled shut; the bottom of the door rubbed slightly in the frame and this proved to be a useful tool for jamming it closed. I sat on the floor opposite him, the penlight torch playing along the lines of text in the latest Harry Potter novel that I was reading to him. I couldn't make out the expression on his face through the darkness that the narrow light hardly infringed upon but it was apparent that his head was tilted to one side.

Was he actually listening to me?

Every night when I removed the motorcycle helmet he was twitchy and seemingly anxious until I had fed him. However, he made that monotonous 'MMMMM' noise less and less. I had started reading to him by mistake. I had just meant to sit with him and had taken my book with me. Without realising what I was doing I had found myself speaking the words out loud and from the first paragraph it seemed to have a calming effect. The genre of book made no difference; I had to assume that it was the sound of his old life that was having this particular impact upon Danny. I sat with my knees raised, the book balanced on them, one hand fingering the pages over, the other holding the tiny torch, my back against the wooden side of the shed. I'd often just stand and look at him for a while, trying to see past those cold, dead eyes. It seemed as if he had paid attention for a while, studying me in reply but had then began to pad forward and back until I opened the book to our last passage and, with a short recap, began to read. The torch dipped a couple of times as my hand grew limp and tired, my eyelids growing heavy, so, with a shake of my head to rouse myself a little, I marked our place in the book and pushed it into the corner, lifting myself to my feet with the torch gripped in one hand.

'Sorry, Danny, I'm too tired', I said, walking around him and picking up the motorcycle helmet.

I sniffed at it and recoiled at the stench. I would have to either clean it or get Danny a new one. The torch lit only a small circle on the back of his neck as I gently eased the helmet over his crown. The skin there was pale and flaky, the bones beneath pressing tightly against it as if they may break through at any moment.

'Good night, Danny', I whispered, as I did every night when I went through this procedure.

'MMMM' he replied, and then it sounded like something got stuck in his throat.

I could have sworn that he said 'Ed.'

'What the heck?' I stumbled backwards and only stopped when I bumped into the wall of the shed.

'What did you say?'

He turned his head a little, as if trying to see me behind him. Again, that half choking, half clearing his throat sound.

And then, more clearly this time, 'Ed.'

21.

As soon as the mobile phone that I had been ignoring stopped ringing then the house phone began. It had reached the point where every time I saw 'Nick' come up as the incoming call, I could not bring myself to answer it. The phone continued to ring, and I finally relented and snatched it up.

'Hello?'

'Matt, Nick here. Listen…'

'Nick, I'm not going. I…'

I had been invited to an awards ceremony to receive medals for what Danny and I had done to rescue those people. I thought the whole thing was a joke and wanted no part of it.

'No, I'm not talking about that. Are you watching the news?'

'No'

'Then turn it on. They're explaining what happened, you won't…'

I hung up on him, grabbed the remote control and switched on the television to the trusty BBC. The newscaster was immaculately dressed, his tie perfectly contrasting his pristinely ironed shirt. It was a giant step away from how the news had been updated during the epidemic. I sat on the arm of the sofa and focussed on the report.

'... have now accepted full responsibility for what was meant to have been a terrorist attack on the United Kingdom. The evidence found in a farm house in the United States, just north of New York, detailed the plot and, as has been previously reported, bodies were found that contained the same toxin which was discovered in each and every victim of the epidemic here.'

This was nothing new. What had gotten Nick so agitated?

'Computer files extracted from the farmhouse have indicated that the toxin was to be transported to Britain in small quantities by around twenty five different individuals. Once the toxin was brought together as a whole, it was to be added to the London water reserves and via this would have been introduced to the general population. Experts who have analysed both the toxin and the files have ascertained that when diluted, the effect would have been to make the population of London docile and listless. The terrorists would then have engaged upon a bombing spree across the capital, meeting with minimum resistance. The scope of the disaster would have been massive.'

The reporter took a breath, and I wondered if this was to give us, the viewers, an opportunity to take in what had been said.

'It has been suggested that the toxin was being carried in a number of different ways and that on the particular flight from New York to London that precipitated the epidemic, it would appear that whatever vessel was being used was damaged and the toxin leaked out. According to the details extracted from the farm house, direct contact with the toxin had not been properly tested, but the end result has had more impact than the terrorists could possibly have hoped for. More details are emerging on almost an hour to hour basis, so we will keep you as informed as we are. Once again…'

This was unbelievable. It was being reported in such a matter of fact way but this had all happened as part of a terrorist plot. What was our Government's reaction to it going to be? I thought back to the footage I had seen right back at the start of the outbreak; the woman in Liverpool and the business man at Heathrow. They must have been on that flight. Had it been in the terrorist's hand luggage, within the legal limits for liquid on a flight? Made to look like after shave, or toothpaste or who knows what? The container must have been breached in some way, broken? And then what? It didn't matter if it had been inhaled or absorbed through the skin; the full strength of the toxin had attached itself to a human host and the rest was almost the total breakdown of our civilisation. The phone rang again. I knew it would be Nick but ignored it anyway.

I now saw what as I was doing as more than trying to save my brother; it was an act of defiance against the terrorists and now I felt more vindicated in protecting Danny's existence out there in the shed than ever before. It was what he would have wanted.

22.

I'd spent the morning with my brother but now locked the shed carefully in anticipation of Nick's arrival. He'd phoned the previous evening and asked if it was okay if he came by at noon the next day. I had not seen much of him, but to be truthful, I had not seen much of anybody. I was sick of the questions and the stares. It was easier to have the shopping delivered, to be by myself than it was to eat out or go to the pub. When I did see Nick, it was more often than not in the pub, and that had been one of the reasons why I had made myself available to see him at home. As had become my habit when I was expecting visitors, I waited on the driveway so I would be able to open the gates for them upon their arrival. I didn't like the idea of leaving them wide open. It wasn't just the aftermath of the epidemic that had bred that into me but the fear that a nosy neighbour, or worse the newspapers, would take their prying a step too far. Cars passed in both directions and although the rain had stopped they still cast up spray from the road. The dark clouds overhead promised another downpour was due but for now it held off and the temperature was warm enough with those clouds acting as a layer of insulation. A car approached from the right and I could tell it was slowing so made my way to the gates, pulling them inwards. Nick waved from the driver's seat and parked with the front of his Citroen facing the garage doors. I closed the gates over behind him and walked, feet slipping on the wet gravel, back towards the front door.

'Kids not with you?' I asked as he locked his car.

'No. Not today. They wanted to come but I need to talk to you alone', he replied.

'This sounds ominous. Is everything okay?'

'It will be.'

I opened the door and let Nick step in ahead of me. We sat at the kitchen table and I offered him a tea, a coffee and after two refusals, a proper drink.

He still said no. He just sat with his hands flat on the table, head looking down into his lap. He had me worried. Had he been out to visit when I wasn't expecting him? Had he seen me going into the shed with a bowl full of raw meat? Had he investigated further?

'Jenny's gone, Matt. She left us three months ago. I've been making excuses why she isn't around but she's gone.'

'What? Gone where?'

'I don't know. She calls every now and then, but that's got less over the weeks. Mate, I had to tell someone. And after what we went through together…'

This bond again. I had every sympathy for him up to that point. Now I could totally comprehend why Jenny had upped and left. What I couldn't understand though was how she could leave her children.

'How're the kids taking this?'

'They're okay. Thanks, mate. They miss her, obviously and ask a million questions a day about whether she'll be coming back. My parents are visiting and they'll stay a while, I hope. I've had to miss quite a bit of work.'

I did the only thing I was capable of doing to help the situation.

'How're you fixed for money?'

'What? No. That's not why I came here.'

'Nick, listen. That I do know. But if you've missed work and Jenny's wage isn't coming in, well I can only guess the extra pressure you're under.'

'My parents have helped a bit but... Are you sure?'

'Yeah, yeah. Just give me a minute.'

I left the kitchen and passed through the lounge to my father's study. I took my cheque book from the desk drawer, glancing up at the polished sword now once again hanging from the wall. I wrote the cheque out quickly and tore the slip off. I walked back into the kitchen and placed it face down on the table.

'Look. It's there, it's not a hassle. End of conversation. Okay?'

'I don't know what to say. After all you've done...'

'Right. That's what you can do. You can stop saying thanks and...'

He had dropped his forehead to rest on his hands.

'And you can please not cry.'

He actually laughed at that, standing up and giving me a hug.

'You'll be okay. Come on. Let's have that drink.'

And an hour later, when he left, I felt better. I had talked to him about how things were for him and the children and I think that was more cathartic than the cheque for both of us. I waved him off at the gate, pushing them shut as he pulled away.

Danny stank. There was no other way to describe it. He reeked of a combination of body odour and, although I hated to admit it, decay. What remained of his right shoulder still oozed a sticky brown puss every now and again, especially when the weather was hot. I wasn't sure if he was going to the toilet in his leather trousers but I honestly didn't think so; the smell would have been ten times worse if he had been. His cheek bones were massively pronounced, as I was sure his jaw would have been too if it was still properly attached to his face. His skin was chalk white. The grey birds' eggs that had replaced his eyes were riddled with tiny red lines and could almost warrant being described as blood shot. For over six months I had fed him and talked to him and read to him and he was calmer and more subdued on a month to month basis. He no longer tried to snatch at the meat with his damaged mouth and when I spoke to him, I genuinely believed that his body language, the tilt of his head to the side, meant that he understood most of what was going on.

'We had a funeral for you', I told him. 'The Government said it would help. I even had to sign a piece of paper to say they could properly dispose of your body. Says something about the amount of bodies over there, doesn't it? Not even Mister Efficient Government Man Mister Penny knew your body wasn't over there. I shouldn't be mean about him. He was nice. He was the one who suggested the funeral. Sion and Rhodri came. People liked you, Danny. They always did.'

I rambled to him as he watched me through those dead eyes. I cut his once white t-shirt off him and threw it to the floor. Even in the pale light that permeated the shed, it was clear that my brother was in a bad way. His ribs stood out through his tight, translucent skin. When I walked behind him I could count every single one of his vertebrae. There was hardly any muscle and no fat to speak of; Danny was wasting away in front of me.

'I'm just going to clean you up a little, okay? Because let's face it, you smell bad.'

'Ed' he slurred, letting his weight sag forward on his emaciated left arm. I pulled the sodden brush out of the bucket and began to scrub his body. The water ran down his chest, over his stomach and down inside the leather motorbike trousers that were literally hanging off him.

'Ed' he said again.

No matter how much or how little I fed him, he still lost weight. I was convinced that if I upped the amount I was giving him then he would start to look more, well, more human. But instead he continued to fade away. In the darkest of night times I believed that he was in fact rotting from the inside out, like he was host to a huge tumour that was draining his body of its vital nutrients.

'Ed.'

'Oh shut up!' I snipped, picked up the bucket and threw its contents straight into his face. He didn't blink. He didn't become aggressive. He just hung there still, feet stepping forward and back on the wet wood. The water dripped from his face and what was left of his hair stood up on end like he had styled it for a night out. I tossed the empty bucket against the side of the shed and dropped to my knees, jeans soaking up some of the soapy water as it ran across the floor. I still held the brush in one hand. Danny's head drooped as he looked down at me. He made a sound I hadn't heard him make before. I couldn't believe it.

'What did you say? What did you say?'

He continued to stare at me blankly, head moving from side to side. And then he uttered the noise again.

'Dah' he repeated, much more clearly.

Nearly seven months I had kept him in here, hoping there would be some way to bring my brother back, and now he was trying to say 'Danny.'

23.

Reading to Danny, even with the battery powered lamp I kept in the shed now, had become a complete chore. It wasn't that I didn't want to do it anymore or even that I thought he no longer responded to the words but he was just more and more vocal during the time I spent in his shed. I would read less than a paragraph and he would start telling his own story back to me. The 'Dah' word had become clearer although on times it sound more like 'Duh.' Either way, he would finish the word with what sounded like a long and drawn out exhalation and I started to believe that he was going to soon add another syllable onto the end of it. So I would start reading, and he would start trying to form his name. And I would put the book down and stand up and try to coach him to say 'Danny.' I could see the frustration in him. He would say 'Dah' or 'Duh' and I would finish the name for him,

'Nee', but as time went on he would shake his head, step towards me, eyes staring right at me as he almost stamped his feet. I wondered if this is how stroke patients or people who had severely injured their spines felt; they could think the words and actions they wanted to carry out but their bodies would not let them fulfill them. So I would calm him down, return to the book and again he would interrupt.

But I still did it. He was my brother and I wanted him to remain as close to human as was possible. For me, a big part of this was not fully looking at him, because when I did I struggled to describe what I saw as my brother Danny. I just had to believe that he was in there still. I had turned to Shakespeare's Macbeth as something that I remembered had caught his attention in school, hoping it would stimulate him now as it had then. It seemed to have worked. He stood absolutely still, left arm loose despite being tied to the rafter, head sloping forward but eyes, as ever, wide open. I finished a scene and as I turned the page I glanced up at him. He had become more alert and was now looking at me.

'You like this story, don't you?' I asked him, finding the words on the top of the new page.

'Duh' he said, and then that breathless sound.

'Yeah, you're Dan…'

'Ed!' he stated, more clearly than ever before.

'Duh – nee, duh – nee', I encouraged. I laid the book down, text to the floor so I didn't lose our page and lifted myself onto my feet.

'You okay there, Danny?'

'Duh… Ed.' He made a motion with his head that made it seem like he was looking himself up and down.

'Duh… Ed' he repeated.

With lifeless, soulless eyes he stared into my face, made the head gesture again.

'Duh… Ed.' The voice, more pleading this time and the tears that fell from my eyes were born of understanding.

212

'Duh…Ed'

He was not saying Ed. He was not trying to say Danny. He was trying to tell me something else, and had been for a long time.

My brother was telling me that he wanted to be dead.

24.

I still held the typed sheet of paper in my hand as I stepped out through the kitchen door and onto the decking. There were very few letters I bothered to open anymore, especially anything that looked official. Most of the other mail that dropped through the letter box were either bills or bank statements, so when the personalised stationary of one of the local solicitor's arrived, it caught my attention. I stood at the bottom of the stairs and peeled open the top flap and after reading just the first paragraph had to put my hand on the banister to steady myself. I couldn't believe what I was reading; the land to the right hand side of our home had been sold to property developers and planning permission had been sought to build apartments. I walked through the house in a daze, unable to formulate any real course of action. The air was warm as I stood looking out over the garden. I was reminded of the day we were told our parents had died and how emptiness had filled me up, had overtaken me.

***

'I'm sorry, Matt, but there's very little we'll be able to do about this. The previous owner had the zoning of the land changed to residential a long time ago and because of where the apartments are going to be positioned, they aren't actually going to be overhanging your property.'

Ram Morjaria had been our family solicitor for years; he'd been the guide for Dad when he set up the copyright on his design and had, with the financial aspects at least, been there for Danny and me after our parents were killed. I trusted him and I knew that he would not only give me the best advice for dealing with this situation but would also go that extra mile if it was at all possible.

'How much will it cost to fight this?'

'You and I both know that the cost isn't the issue, Matt. The point is that no matter how much we dig in our heels, all we're going to be able to do is slow them down. We can't stop them.'

Ram ran his hand across his white beard, shaking his head as he did so. He was a tall, slightly built man. His Indian accent had softened over the years and he'd developed a light Welsh lilt on certain words.

'Matt, did you not see the Council's notices?'

I shrugged.

'Matt, they would have been up on the lamp posts, telegraph poles over the last few months? You would have even received a letter? Do you not recall any of this?'

'I've just been wrapped up in my own life. I haven't paid much attention to stuff, well not since…'

Ram stood up and came around to my side of his desk.

216

'I'll see what I can do, but I cannot promise anything. As I said, all I think we can do is slow this down. And maybe if enough barriers are put in the way, then maybe the project will just fade away. But don't hold out too much hope.'

'Trust me', I said, getting to my feet and shaking his hand. 'I don't hold out too much hope for anything anymore.'

How could I? I had no choice now but to fulfil my brother's wish.

25.

Dusk had become night by the time I finished digging. Blisters had formed and split on each hand and a thick, muddy sweat ran down into my eyes. I rubbed the back of my hand across my forehead and held it there as the tears came again. I thrust the blade of the shovel into the soil and then used it to hold me upright until I could drag myself back together. I knew this had to happen at some point, but I wasn't ready. I couldn't finish this, not now, not tonight.

I had chosen the plot well. It was in the corner of the back garden, tight in by the six foot wall that had been, for what seemed like the longest time, the only thing that had stood between us and the end. I'd planted a row of saplings that would give this spot even more cover. I of course had kidded myself at the time that it was the best place for them to catch the sun, and that the rain water drained away towards that corner too. But I knew what I was doing and why. That once Danny told me he wanted to die that it would have to come to this.

I needed to go into the shed. The roll of plastic pond liner was in there. It was as much as I could do to open the door and throw it in there last week. Why hadn't I just left it in the garage? No chance could I open that door now and face the full extent of what was needed to finish this once and for ever. Leaving the shovel standing upright, I climbed the ladder out of the hole. It was at least three foot deep and three foot wide. I would double line it with the plastic sheeting and then dump him in; simple as that but not now. A shuffling sound came from inside the shed. Could I hear that shallow, raspy breathing or was it an echo in my mind?

'Shut up', I muttered, unsure.

Head bowed I began the trek up to the house.

***

I let the water run until the shower was hot. My skin stung as I washed the dirt off myself, rinsed the suds and turned the shower off. Hearing the telephone ring I stepped out of the shower cubicle, quickly took a towel from the silver heated towel rail and wrapped it around my waist, a habit I would never lose no matter how long I lived by myself.

'Hello.'

'Matt? This is Nick. How are you, mate?'

I could do without this. I had complete sympathy for him, I really did, but I had enough on my mind tonight and I couldn't cope with his issues too.

' Look, I've just got out of the shower and…'

'Okay, I get the message, mate. But I'll be in the King's Head for last orders if you fancy it. You know where I am.'

Yeah, more and more in the pub, mate.

'Appreciate it, Nick', I said possibly a little too sarcastic, 'Sorry. Just tired.'

'Not a worry, mate. I'll catch you soon.'

Click.

I sat on the edge of the bed and placed the phone back in its cradle.

What do I say to him?

Sorry, would love a pint but just been digging a grave in my back garden?

My stomach rumbled and I knew I needed to eat, but fatigue overtook me and I slumped onto the bed. I desperately tried to keep my eyes open, because every time I closed them all I could see was Danny's face.

***

I must have drifted off at some point, fading in and out of sleep without gaining any of the real benefit. I could feed myself all kinds of rubbish that it was bad dreams that kept me awake but I didn't think I ever went off deep enough to have nightmares, and if I did, I was lucky that I was unable to recall them. The digital clock on the bedside cabinet said 6:45. I got out of bed and headed downstairs.

The lights remained on in the kitchen but I flicked the switch off as I walked in; the bright March sunshine was burning in around gaps in the curtains and that was more than enough for making coffee. Although my back felt tight and my hands had been better, I was generally as okay as I could be and wanted to press on. The kettle boiled and I added the hot water to the coffee. I unlocked the back door and stepped through onto the decking, looking out over the garden. From here I could see over the wall at the end of the property and across the river toward Usk itself. I could see the floodlights from the tennis club and beyond that the cricket field. Further away, and to the left, was the steeple of the church, these days more a spiritual centre of the village than it had been in decades.

The garden was nicely laid out, the decking, a long stretch of lawn with a pond in the middle, the large shed off to the left and in the far left corner, the row of saplings and the hole I had created the evening before. That kind of ruined the scene. Over the left wall was the neighbours' expansive garden, bigger than ours, so much so that their house was far enough away not to overlook even a section of our land. To the right had been farm fields, now sold, and it was my final failure to get the plans rejected that had brought me to this dark and miserable place.

I finished my coffee and a small bowl of cereal before pulling on some clothes and finally my boots. I felt my stomach churn as I purposefully marched down the garden with the keys to the shed in my hand. The shovel had tilted in the night and lay against the side of the hole but the ladder was just as I had left it. The hole was deep enough and I couldn't keep putting this off. I unlocked the two padlocks on the shed and leaned in. There was immediate movement and a muffled gasp, almost a moan, but I blocked out all aural intrusions and I was able to pull out the roll of plastic pond liner without any trouble. I pushed the shed door closed and launched the roll down into the hole, turned and re-clipped the padlocks and pushed the keys to the bottom of my pocket. I climbed down the ladder, stopping halfway as a muscle in my back gave a small twinge. Pulling the shovel out of the ground, I threw it up over the lip of the hole, only then realising how fatigued my deltoids were. The shovel almost made it, but then tumbled back down toward me. If I wasn't so tired I could have jumped out of the way, but I didn't and the blade caught me a glancing blow on the right forearm, bringing up a narrow line of blood. Immediately, I wiped it off then let it well up again. I glanced at the shed door.

'Shut up', I said coldly, looking down at my wound.

Not so long ago a cut like that would be a death sentence but now I had no need to worry and it could be cleaned and dressed later. This time, I climbed halfway back up the ladder before popping the shovel up onto the level ground, laying the ladder flat in the hole after I had stepped back down. I unrolled the pond liner as best I could, doubling it over and folding it up the sides of the hole. I used the ladder to weigh down the liner while I folded and adjusted it, then righted it and ascended for the last time. The keys were burning a hole in my pocket. I could do this now. No one could see me; I had checked every angle, had even trespassed on my neighbours grounds to check if they could see anything until their black Labrador had spotted me and brought its ball over for me to throw. It had felt good, to do something normal. Not like doing this. I had to be sensible. Yes, everything was set to go; now I would have to wait until darkness began to fall later in the evening. I had to sort out the cut on my arm and then find something to keep me occupied.

***

The night had a crisp, cold bite and I knew that the bottle of vodka sat at my side was not helping me get any warmer. It wasn't making me feel any better either; it was taking me to a darker place than the one I was already in. Like that was possible. My plan had been to eat, have a couple of slugs of booze to increase my confidence and then get the job done. I didn't drink much but a few shots had turned to half the bottle and before I had taken up camp on the decking, I had phoned Nick and arranged to meet him tomorrow. I sat staring out across the garden, the pond, over to the hole, the grave I had dug. A short while earlier a cat had slunk across the lawn to the pond, lapped at the water and then strutted off. I couldn't recall the last time I had seen an animal in our garden. Birds didn't even linger for too long. The trees between the furthest reaches of the boundary wall and the river trembled in the light wind that had picked up, silhouetted by the orange glow from the town. The sky wasn't totally clear of cloud and although the moon was covered, a spattering of bright stars glistened brightly above me. I still had one other job to finish tonight. I tried to push myself up off the decking. I had to do it and the first thing I needed were the shed keys. I didn't even get half way up before losing my balance a little and I slumped back to the floor, knocking over the vodka bottle. It rolled away from me, rotating slowly as it went, trailing the alcohol in looping letters like when we were first taught joined up writing in the classroom.

I got to my feet with a struggle and picked up the now static vodka bottle. I took a mouthful and stepped back towards the house. I stole a look at the shed. There was no sound from there tonight, but there never was during darkness. I wouldn't have been able to handle that. Since the end of the epidemic I had felt no fear but if I ever heard a howl in the middle of the night, it would drag me back to those terrifying days when it felt the world was on the cusp of capitulation. I stepped into the kitchen and pulled the door shut behind me. All the lights in the rooms I used were, as ever, on. I paused at the kitchen table, sank a little more vodka, cradled the bottle in my arms and headed towards the front of the house. I stood unsteadily and unsure at the foot of the stairs. I took each step upwards slowly and methodically. With the shuffling steps of a drunk I reached the door to Danny's room.

How long was it since I had stepped inside?

Too long.

And I couldn't bring myself to do it now, not when the only thought coursing through my mind was about how I was going to kill my brother.

26.

Beeping.

Not loud, but not going away either.

Wanting to sleep just a little longer.

Head hurting.

Louder

Mobile phone. Ringing. My mobile phone ringing.

My mobile was on the bedside cabinet, screen flashing, ringing.

I reached for it.

I touched the green button and put the phone to my ear, glad just to have silenced the sound that was drilling a hole into my head.

'Hello.'

'Matt mate, it's Nick.'

Who else?

'Matt, can you hear me?'

'Yeah, I'm here.'

'Okay, cool. Look, I'll pick you up at twelve, save you leaving your car in town overnight.'

Oh man, I could do without this today, I had something to do. I'd forgotten I'd arranged to meet him but then I'd planned it when I thought the last place I'd want to be today was at home.

'Is that okay for you?', then slightly more coldly. 'You're still planning on coming aren't you, mate?'

'Yeah, yeah, sorry. Just woke up. That's fine. I'll see you then. And Nick? Thanks.'

'Not a worry. See you in an hour', and he hung up.

I showered and dressed quickly into loose, light blue jeans and my Wales rugby shirt. I gathered yesterday's filthy clothes into a bundle and headed down the stairs. Having dumped them into the washer, I popped on the kettle and opened the back door. It was a beautiful morning and the cat was back at the pond, batting the water with a black and white paw as if trying to entice a fish to the surface.

I watched it play until the kettle boiled and as I spooned coffee into a cup I heard a car pull across the gravel drive at the front of the house. I closed the back door and flicked the lock, then pulled the blinds down over the door and drew the curtains over the windows. I could hardly keep Nick waiting outside but I didn't want him to see the new addition to the back garden, and I didn't mean the cat. I set another coffee cup ready and made my way to the front door. Half way there, Nick knocked and it was only then I realised how tense I had been as I jumped out of my skin. I opened the door, beckoned for him to follow me into the kitchen, where I lifted the kettle and poured the water into the cups, added milk from the fridge, stirred and passed him his drink without even a word.

'You look like...' his smile faltered briefly. 'Oh, mate. Heavy night? I didn't think you liked drinking.'

I took a swig of coffee and nodded, 'I don't, but I'll be okay for today. If you can't pick it for a couple of beers with a mate, when can you?

'That's what I want to hear. Hey, and thanks for opening the gate for me, that must have been a bit too much like hard work on a Saturday morning for you, mate.'

'Uh? Oh, no worries.'

I'd left the gate open? I hadn't done that since, well, probably never. Not that it was such a life or death issue anymore but still not like me at all.

We drank our coffee in silence.

'You set?'

'Yeah, sure', I put my cup straight into the sink, took my keys, wallet and mobile phone off the counter and slid them into my pockets.

We headed out to his car, the same Citroen he and his family had pulled up in all that time ago.

Nick hardly stopped talking all of the way into town. The kids were doing great, holding their own at school and taking part in a variety of sports and activities. His parents were looking after them today, as they did often these days, but most importantly, the children didn't seem to mind. He hadn't mentioned Jenny and I wasn't going to ask. I don't know how I would have reacted had he been the one to bring the subject up but questioning him outright on the breakup of his marriage would have been insensitive.

'So, how are things with you?'

I looked out of the window. The sky was clear and blue, making the day look warmer than it felt..

'Matt?'

'Sorry,' I replied, winding down the window. 'I'm okay. Not really done much, but then, when do I?'

'We need to get you out more, mate. Come over for dinner soon. The kids would love that.'

'You know what? Next week, I might just do that. I got a couple of things to take care of and then I'll be back to normal.'

Nick left the car in the main car park in the centre of town and it was just after half past twelve when we entered the King's Head. I laid a twenty pound note down on the bar as we sat down on a couple of the tall stools and Nick swigged down about half of his pint in one go. My first mouthful tasted disgusting but the second and third got better and we finished at about the same time. Nick signalled the barman 'same again' and pulled out his wallet, opening it to reveal a photo of himself, Jenny and the kids. He saw me notice and shrugged.

'Can't let go, mate', he said as he passed some money over the bar. 'But look, are you okay? If this is all too much...'

'No, I'm fine. But what about you? I never ask, but seeing...' I gestured towards his wallet. 'I kind of forget, you know.'

'Nah, well, I don't exactly bring it up myself.' He paused, took another long drink, 'And today ain't about all that anyway, is it? Let's not drag ourselves down by bringing up the past, mate.' He brought his glass to mine with a clink and smiled at me in a way that told me this conversation was over. Please.

'Too right.' I tapped my glass against his this time. Maybe he did realise how much the past hurt after all. But he could have no idea just how close my past was still.

***

I edged my way back from the bar, politely requesting a clear passage to our table, the two pints of lager in my hands spilling slightly as I was jostled. I placed them down on the table and wiped my hands on the back of my jeans.

'Sorry', I told Nick. 'Got talking to a couple of people.'

'Well what do I expect?' asked Nick, lifting his beer off the table and taking a huge mouthful. 'If I'm going to have lunch with a local celebrity, what else is going to happen?'

I shrugged, uncomfortable with the tag with which Nick had labelled me. The King's Head had filled up quickly after we had arrived and we ended up eating our burgers and chips in the main bar. I was glad to eat; the drinking pace had if anything picked up and I was starting to feel less than perfect. I was also concerned that the more beer that went down my neck, the more the urge to confess everything to Nick rose to the surface of my mind.

Would he understand what I had done?

Well, he'd been with us through it all. That was one thing. But had he suffered the loss that I had? Okay, Jenny had left him and the kids afterwards but that was down to their relationship. It wasn't the same. I was drawn out of my thoughts when Steve, the landlord, approached our table. He extended his hand to me and shook it.

'Good to see you, Matt', he said. 'Could you boys do me a favour and sit through in the other room? I've got diners queued up out of the door and

I've put the football on in the function room for the residents so dinner tables are at a premium.'

'Sure', I said, taking to my feet and picking up my pint glass.

'Who's playing?' asked Nick, not moving.

'I don't know', shrugged Steve. 'But I've opened the bar in there.'

'Come one, Nick', I said, nodding my head towards the door.

***

'I know you', Tommo said, leaning forward with one elbow on the table, a thick index finger pointing my way. I heard Nick sigh. The bar was busy and we had been forced to share a table with three people neither of us knew. I was too drunk to remember all of their names but Tommo was huge and hard to forget. He also kept staring at me.

'No, I don't think so', I replied with a smile.

'I'm sure I do', he nodded, the seriousness dropping out of his face. 'It'll come to me.'

'I'm going to the toilet', said Nick and got up, knocking the table with his knees. Without apologising he headed for the loo.

'I'm going for some air', I said, my stomach starting to churn up the alcohol with the food.

I walked down the narrow corridor to the front door of the pub. The rain that had held off all day was now falling in a light mist.

'Mind if I join you?'

I turned round to see Tommo in the doorway.

'No worries.'

He stood next to me, leaning back against the wall.

'I knew I knew you', he nodded. 'From what I recall, you went through Hell.'

'Sorry?'

It felt like he was angling to start a conversation about what happened in Usk during the epidemic and as I was about to divert the topic, he surprised me by taking the initiative with his own story.

'I lost my wife.' He paused, almost gave me a chance to say sorry, or one of the many platitudes I had received over the last year. 'I was working in Saudi at the time. Me and Kevin, my mate inside, were over there. When I first heard bout what was going on, I thought Aberdeen was far enough north to be safe, you know, what with the flight coming into Heathrow and all? But someone jumped a connection and there it was. She died outright, so they told me. Didn't. You know. Become like them. I'd tried to get home, but there was no chance.'

He paused for the longest time.

'And I gave myself a hard time for a long time. I'll tell you that. Because I wasn't there. But what could I have done? Would she still be alive? Maybe, but I doubt it. And I'd be gone too. At least I am around to remember her. Just like you are for who you lost, and for the rest of the people in this town that you knew.'

He stopped and straightened himself up from the wall.

'I'm sorry' I said, and meant it.

He nodded and walked back inside the pub. Maybe all the people who'd said how sorry they were to me had meant it. Had I been so wrapped up in all that had gone on and had continued to go on in my life to notice that other people did actually care? That the good things I had done and tried to achieve had made an impact upon people? That by shunning Nick I was actually…

'It's always about you, isn't it?'

I turned to see Nick in the doorway.

'Matt, the hero. Matt, the martyr. You weren't the only one who lost someone you know.'

'Nick, I…'

'Everyone wants to talk to you. A quick word, a shake of the hand. Everyone remembers your story. It's like I wasn't even there. Well, I'll tell you something, mate, I've had enough.'

I didn't know what to say as he walked towards me and shoved me in the chest with both hands. I stumbled backwards but kept my balance.

'Nick! This isn't you. Leave it.'

'Shut it!' he shouted.

'Nick. What the hell is wrong with you?'

'Wrong with me? Wrong with me?' he stepped towards me. 'What's wrong with you? After all that went on, it's like you exist in your own little bubble.'

'What the heck? Look, we've both had too much to drink and I know…'

'You know nothing. Nothing.'

He turned and started walking away. My head was spinning. The fresh air had actually made me feel more drunk and on another day I would have let him go. I should have let him go. But I didn't. I caught up with him and put my right hand on his shoulder, pulling him around to face me.

'Look…'

I didn't get a chance to finish the sentence. I was sat on the floor with my jaw very sore. Nick stood over me, clasping his left fist with his right hand.

'What's today all about for you, mate? Go for a few beers to keep me sweet, mate? You have no idea what my life is like. You think Jenny left because of me? Is that what you think?' he paused, tears now rolling off his cheeks and dropping to join the mounting rain hitting the floor. 'She left because of you.'

I was totally confused. 'What?'

'Yeah, you. She hated seeing you. She hated me talking about you, talking to you. Because it reminded her of what happened. It reminded her that it was as much her idea as it was Danny's. And when she asked me to save our marriage, to cut you out of our lives, I said no. Because I owed you. For the kids' lives.'

His voice slowed down as he spoke the last two sentences, his arms dropped to his sides. He shook his head and turned, began walking away again.

'Nick, wait,' I started to pick myself up off the ground. 'Nick, I'm sorry. I've been… I…'

'What Matt? What?'

Should I tell him now? Should I explain my behaviour over the last twelve months? I couldn't force the words out of my mouth, and all the noise I made was another pitiful whine.

'I'm sorry.'

'No you're not. You're not, because now I won't bother you any more. Good luck. Mate.'

I let myself sit back down. I could have got up. I could have shouted to him. I could have chased after him. I could have let him take another swing at me. I could have told him the truth. But I didn't.

I gave Nick a good five minutes head start and then began walking in the same direction. The proper thing for me to do was to follow him and sort this out now. Apologise and mean it. Tell him the truth. If what he had said about Jenny leaving him had been true, then he must have been building up to that like a pressure cooker on low heat. And the way I fobbed him off, not just the manner I had often taken with him, but the number of times I had just made up blatant lies and excuses not to have anything to do with him, none of that could have helped.

I ran through how I could approach things with Nick. First up would be an apology. No doubt about that. Then to try to rebuild things? Is that what I wanted? Not really, and trying to solve this drunk was going to get me nowhere. All I knew for certain was that I couldn'tt tell him the real reason for my behaviour. What kind of reaction would I get if I just blurted it all out? He would be... I don't know. I had misjudged him once already today and look where that had gotten me. And, now, did it matter anymore? Was I just dealing with the guilt I was feeling for Nick or was I feeling it for Danny? My brain wasn't able to deal with the messages pinging about from one side of my head to the other. The evening was now night as the final daylight faded from the sky. The orange glow of the street lamps cast warped fire-like reflections across the damp road. With no jacket to keep me warm, and having first checked that I still had my wallet, keys, and phone, I jammed my hands into my jeans pockets and started to walk up towards Bridge Street.

I stood on the corner looking left and right. Right would take me up towards Nick. Left was the way home, past the hairdressers', over the bridge and the long march up the road. Talking to Nick tonight was out of the question. The rain intensified. Before I knew it, I was alone and half way over the bridge, I paused and looked down into the River Usk. It chopped and swirled and was both deeper and faster flowing than I had seen it in a long time. It was a thick, dark moving mass of water that looked to have several lives of its own as it separated around the bottoms of the arches that kept the bridge up. The evening had gotten so grim that I could hardly make out the shape of the railway bridge just a few hundred yards upstream. The back of my jeans got splashed as a car passed behind me, heading into Usk. I took that as my sign to press on and get myself home as quickly as possible.

Everything seemed darker and it was not just due to the clouds that blocked out every inch of sky; a huge part of the darkness came from inside me and impinged upon the way I was seeing everything. The rain had made the greens of the grass richer yet more sinister. The thought processes going through my drunken and angry mind were a paranoid knot of denial and confusion. Even as my brain played through the events of the last few days I could feel the water ooze between my toes as my shoes filled more with every step either into a puddle or onto the banking to avoid approaching vehicles. Had Jenny really felt that she held some responsibility for what had happened? Was it right that I had done what I had done, yet never told them? What if I had been able to share with Nick and Jenny how I had tried to right things? Would it have made any difference to their relationship?

My rugby shirt clung to my back and at times I could barely make out the road ahead as the rain and growing wind buffeted me. A couple of times I was totally blinded by the headlights of cars coming towards Usk from Caerleon. On more than one occasion, a truck or lorry gave me a blast of its horn as it got nearer; double checking that I was actually going to get out of the way.

What right did she have, anyway? Guilt was my issue, Danny was my brother. Yeah, if she had issues with her marriage, she should deal with them. Don't be looking for some scapegoat, someone you can shift the blame to.

I was soaking wet before I had even reached the rugby club, but having walked past the garden centre and into the cover of the first proper road side copse of trees I paused in the relative shelter for a few minutes. Hardly any traffic passed while I was stood there, droplets of rain dripping from the end of my nose. As I started walking again I realised that I was not just soaked but also incredibly muddy. My jeans were filthy right up to the knees and as I plodded, now weaving in the road slightly as the fresh air and the alcohol combined again, I considered that if I was this dirty, I might as well get it done now. Just crack on and do it. Was I drunk enough that I wouldn't remember it all in the morning? Probably not. But I was drunk enough that I wouldn't remember all of it. As I passed the entrance to my neighbour's house, to Des's place, I realised that this was something I could do, something I should do. Put all this business to bed forever tonight. Leave it all behind me. Get up tomorrow, suffer the hangover of both the drinking and the fall out with Nick. Sort things with him. Have it all out. Tell him straight about a few things but, 'ha ha', the irony, take it on the chin from him too. The wall to my house began to stand out prominently in the gloom as I came nearer and when I finally reached the gates, I pushed the left side open and stepped inside. The sound of my footsteps changed from a squelch to a crunch as the wet gravel shifted under my feet. I slipped to the floor, managing to remember to release my grip on the gates as I fell. My hands were feeling a great deal better but if I was going to do this, there was no reason to injure them further at this stage. I was going to do this. Now. Using the gate, I hauled myself to my feet, and with my current lack of balance, had to swing it even wider open in order to get myself into a standing position. I pulled my house keys out of the pocket of my sodden jeans. After a few failed attempts I finally unlocked the front door and stumbled into the house, slamming the door behind me.

27.

The whole house was in darkness. Without turning on the hall or lounge lights, I strode through to the kitchen, leaving wet, muddy footprints in the carpet as I went. I flicked the light on long enough to unlock the back door and grab the shed keys from their secret place, then once again plunged the house into darkness. I opened the door and stepped out onto the decking. The wood had a newly varnished look because of the amount of rain that had fallen on it and the glare from the motion sensitive light mounted above the back door, but it held no puddles as it was slightly angled so that the grooves in the wood carried the water off towards the garden. I crossed it quickly, treading carefully down the steps, slipped a little as I put my first foot on the grass but didn't fall over. I headed towards the hole I had dug, checking that it hadn't filled too much with water and that the shovel was still at the top where I had left it. Although there was a fair bit of water accumulated on the pond liner, I was not put off. The stuff was waterproof; of course it was going to hold water. And the shovel, also soaked, was right there. I couldn't remember whether I had left it lying on the ground or had tried to keep it upright by thrusting it into the soil. Whatever I had tried to do, it now lay on the ground. The rain kept pounding down, the noises it made when hitting the shed roof, the pond or the lining in the bottom of the hole competing with each other to be the loudest. I'd kept the shed keys tight in my left hand and now I put them to use, unlocking the two padlocks. The first one clicked open easily, so I detached it, opened the hasp and then hooked the arm of the lock over the top of it. The second one took a couple of attempts before it came loose and then I pulled open the door. I paused for a couple of seconds. Everything I needed to complete my task was just inside the shed. Easily accessible, even in the dark. I turned a complete three hundred and sixty degree circle, looking for any sign that I was being observed. Even though I overbalanced and stumbled towards the hole a little I was able to ascertain that I was in the clear. I gently opened the shed door and stepped inside, pulling it shut behind me, sealing me in darkness.

The sound of the rain hitting the roof was immediately amplified. I could hear Danny's breathing and could smell the stench coming off him. As my eyes got used to the gloom I stood behind him and pulled the motor cycle helmet off his head, letting it drop to the wood floor with a dull thud. He didn't make his usual jerky head movements. I stepped slowly around Danny, concentrating hard on placing one foot in front of the other, on not letting the contents of my stomach spew out of me and all over the floor. I took a deep breath and picked up the sharpened broom stick I had prepared as a stake.

Danny looked at me, his head lolling to the side.

'Duh… Ed.'

He had never been so calm. No longer did his feet work their little dance back and forth. He stared straight at me but there was no malice or vicious intent in those cold, grey eyes. I convinced myself that he knew the time had come and that he was glad of it. I stood directly in front of him, the stake in my right hand. I wasn't yet crying but I knew I would be soon. I had things to say to him first and I prayed that he would understand and that there was enough of my brother still inside that he could forgive me.

'I thought, by keeping you out here, that I could save you. I thought they'd find a way to reverse the effects. But they never will, Danny. And I shouldn't have put you through all of this.'

The tears were now dripping off my nose, off my chin, my cheeks. Danny was silent, just looking at me with that vacant stare.

'But I love you. And I can't let you suffer anymore. I can't let other people find out about you. I need to release you from this.'

'Duh... Ed' he said. And then he raised his chin, squared his head on his shoulders, and very slowly and very deliberately, he nodded his head.

'Duh... Ed.'

I brought the tip of the stake up level with his left eye. My hands were shaking so much that I could hardly bear its weight.

'Duh... Ed' and then he actually pushed his eye towards the sharp wood. He then nodded again.

He was telling me to do it. He was asking me to end his suffering.

And with a moan, both my hands wrapped around the stake in much the same way that my brother had used a sword during the epidemic, I drove the shard through his left eye and into his brain.

Danny went limp before I even withdrew the device of his death. All of his weight was suddenly on the rope holding his arm to the rafters. His knees sagged and the toes of one of his boots slid across the floor in tiny circles. He still looked up at me.

Where his left eye had been was now only a hole; no blood, no body fluids seeping out of the wound but just a hole. His right eye, grey and lifeless as it was, bored a furrow to my soul. I was still holding the stake and I lifted it again. I had to. I couldn't bear him looking at me, accusing me. I had killed my brother and all I wanted to do was die.

I leant down to my left and found the small axe, its handle pointing upwards. I looked up at the thick wooden rafter, at the rope that was tied around it, holding my brother's arm tightly in place above his head. I could only see the top of his head, thank God, and after two, three solid swipes of the axe, the rope first frayed and then gave way, the axe fully imbedded into the rafter. His body fell to the ground with a light thump, nestling in the corner of the shed, legs straight out in front of him, arm hanging limply across his chest, and now, for want of a better phrase, his empty eye sockets staring me straight in the eyes.

28.

Being so drunk had a numbing effect upon me. It pulled me out of my emotional hole and helped me get a grip on myself. I could not draw my gaze away from Danny's face, from where Danny's eyes used to be. The way his head sat on his emaciated shoulders, it truly did seem as if he was returning my stare with a questioning lilt, his right ear almost touching his bare right clavicle. I had ended it for him swiftly, exactly as he had with so many of the infected when they were grouped at our gate, so desperate to feed on us. I hoped I had sent his soul, if it had still been left in this wasted, broken body, to a better place.

I took a step forward towards the body, meaning to start pulling it out of the shed and towards the edge of the hole, the grave I had dug for my brother. I leapt backwards when something brushed against the top of my head. My shoes, wet and caked in mud, lost their traction and I regained my balance only when my shoulders were wedged in the furthest corner of the shed. At least I hadn't fallen over but ridiculously I had my fists up in front of my face, ready to defend myself. Nothing moved in the darkness and I realised I had felt the frayed end of the rope that had held my brother in place touch me. Maybe the alcohol wasn't taking away all of my senses after all. I stepped back across the shed, leant down and gripped the rest of the rope still bound to Danny with both hands. I bent my knees and then gently extended upwards, using them to take the strain and saving my still niggling back muscles. Danny's left arm reached out towards me as the rope tightened and he flopped forward, head settling in between his legs. At least he could no longer stare back at me. I retreated out of the shed, bumping the door open with my right hip and tugging in a slow steady rhythm until Danny was completely out of the shed. By the time I had brought him to the edge of the hole he had left a deep mark along where there had used to be grass but was now, because of the amount of times I had walked over this particular spot, just a muddy mess. His motorbike boots had left two deep ski tracks and his leather biking trousers had been dragged down a few inches. His wasted body must have been about half the weight it was when he was alive and healthy. I released the rope which was now wet and slick and I noticed for the first time that the rain had eased up and was in fact close to stopping. I dropped to one knee and hitched up Danny's trousers as far as I could and then grasping him by what was left of his right shoulder, I rolled him over onto his back.

I looked over Danny's body for the final time. His black boots had thick divots of mud on the toes, the shins smeared and mucky, and his leather trousers were in the same state. The loose waistband had trapped a huge clump of wet, brown earth. His stomach was concave and slight, every single one of his ribs visible through the pale skin. There were no chest muscles to speak of anymore and his left arm was nothing more than skin wrapped tightly around bone. His right arm was no longer there. Only a few inches of the upper arm remained, the skin around it hacked and blackened where whatever blood left in the system had congealed. Smears of mud ran in patches along his skin. The jaw hung slack and loose from when I had been forced to dislocate it and then I simply could not look anymore. This wasn't my brother. This was a shell in which I thought I could find the lost remnants of the boy who was my best friend, who was my family. My tears fell onto the body as I stood over him.

'I love you, Danny', I whispered as I fell to my knees next to him.

I pushed my hands under his hips and shoulders, the slick ground underneath him easily giving way. A car blasted past the front of the house, the only sound I had heard since emerging from the shed and I jumped, a sharp expletive escaping my mouth. I lifted and shoved in one motion, feeling something in my back give way and Danny tumbled over into his grave, landing with a dull thump and a small splash at the bottom of the hole. I stayed down on my knees, hands squeezing the mud between my fingers. The rain had now completely stopped at a time when a heavy downpour coupled with thunder and lightning would have been more fitting to the emotions within me. I gradually got to my feet, the booze not helping me at all anymore. I struggled to breathe, both my eyes and nose a continual running stream. I looked down into the grave and Danny was again lying on his back, his left arm, frayed rope still knotted around the wrist, elevated across his chest.

Should I climb down and lay him out properly with some dignity?

I was kidding myself. There was no dignity in this situation. My brother had died over a year ago. I had been the only one who had not been able to accept that. I picked up the shovel and moved to the end of the grave where Danny's head rested. With quick but inefficient strokes I got my first goal out of the way; I covered his head so he couldn't look up at me with that accusing stare. I worked my way around the grave, throwing the dirt in until he was completely covered, having to pile more in over his feet. I then moved back and forth from the large pile of earth next to the shed until almost a third of the hole was filled in. My hands were bleeding, my rugby shirt filthy and soaking wet. My jeans and shoes would have to go straight into the bin, no doubt about that. I dug the blade of the shovel once again into the mud and as I straightened up I felt my back finally give out. I collapsed onto the floor with a thin whistle of air escaping between my gritted teeth. My lower back muscles tightened up and I knew I was done for the night. I released my grip on the shovel and forced myself to breath deeply. When I finally got to my feet, I walked passed the edge of Danny's grave. Is this what I thought I could have told Nick to make everything better? This made nothing better.

'Goodbye, Bro', I said and began to limp up towards the decking and the back door.

***

Using the banister I dragged myself up the stairs. I would shower and at least lay down on the bed; even if I couldn't sleep it would ease the muscles that were currently screaming at me. My hands had blistered up again and they had burst. My palms burnt and stung and the skin was raw. I should have gone straight to my room, to the hot shower that my body was desperately craving. But instead my feet led me to Danny's door. I turned the handle and pushed the door inwards. Even in the darkness I could see his computer, his shelves, his books and movies. I stepped inside. The television screen mounted on the wall reflected someone I didn't know, someone I did not want to know. I stepped towards it and with both hands, ripped it from the wall. It landed with a crash that made me jump back from it. I then systematically pulled his bookshelves to the floor, casting DVD boxes, C. D.s and novels across the carpet. A sound stopped me; a deep, resonant scream that terrified me. Then I realised it was me. The energy sagged from my body and I felt sick. I was crying again as I closed Danny's bedroom door , only it wasn't Danny's room anymore and never would be again.

THE END

29.

My head hurt far more than my back or my hands. The bedside lamp had burnt all night but now the sun forced its way into my room around the edges of the curtains. I lay naked under the duvet, having shed my shorts and rugby shirt when I'd taken first a hot and then a freezing cold shower before falling backwards onto the bed. At some point I must have dragged the covers over me, but I'd shivered all through the night. Even though I could sense the heat under the duvet, the time spent out in the rain and the task I'd finally undertaken had robbed me of any internal warmth. Acid, brought on by the amount of alcohol I'd drunk, burnt a hole in my stomach. Sitting up was difficult and my lower back screamed at me just to lie down on the floor and stretch out. Instead I pushed myself to my feet, the effort making my head spin, and walked with a limp to the bathroom. I cleaned my teeth and rinsed my mouth out. Had I been sick during the night? I wouldn't have been surprised. I grabbed the towel off the rail and wiped my mouth, letting it fall to the floor when I was finished. Despite how cold I felt, my body, with such little exertion, had broken out in a thin sheen of sweat and I probably needed another shower. That could wait. Another half an hour in the garden and all of this would, physically at least, be behind me. I stepped gingerly back into the bedroom and slid the wardrobe open and selected a pair of grey jogging trousers, possibly one of the items worn by either Susan or Claire when Danny and I had brought them back here, and a light blue Nike sweatshirt. I threw both onto the bed and rooted around in my bedside drawer for clean socks and underwear.

Getting dressed was a slow and uncomfortable process. Every movement of my hands stung, each lean forward to pull on clothing made already strained muscles tighten and jump under my skin, especially when I put on my socks and trainers. With a final effort, I drew the sweatshirt over my head, my left shoulder particularly uncomfortable. I pulled the curtains open, letting the bright sunshine fully invade my room. It was not my most intelligent move as the light cut straight through my eyes into my brain, making it bang even harder around my skull. I blinked a few times and made a mental note that the gate needed to be closed before I finished filling in Danny's grave. I turned away from the window, switched off the bedside lamp and exited my bedroom.

***

I stood at the back door for almost twenty minutes without opening it, my forehead against the cool glass. I finally unlocked the door and stepped out onto the shaded decking. Squinting already, my eyes were drawn to the far right hand corner where the recent guest to the garden, the little black and white cat, crouched on top of the wall, staring over towards the shed. I followed its gaze across the grass, over the pond, to the hole I'd dug and buried my brother in, where there was clearly something moving.

What?

I moved as quickly as I could towards the top of the steps and tried to take them two at a time. My aching body rebelled against me and my lower back completely locked, stealing my balance from me and I plunged the final six or seven steps. I landed on my right shoulder and rolled across the sodden grass. I finished with my left cheek on the floor, looking down the garden at the top of the hole. Something black appeared over the cusp, grew out of the ground and came bounding towards me. Instinctively I closed my eyes and tried to cover my head with my arms and push myself away as it got closer, panting, feet thumping as it sprinted towards me. It got all but on top of me when I opened my eyes and shrieked.

The black Labrador launched itself onto me and nuzzled into my cheek, leaving a thick blob of drool which ran down into my mouth. I pushed the animal off, spitting onto the grass to get rid of the disgusting taste of dog slobber. The Labrador sat in front of me, trying to give me its front right paw. I could feel my heart banging inside my chest but I took first the right and then the left paw, checking between the nails and mud for any evidence of Danny's flesh. The dog seemed clear but even so it was happy to let me push its saggy cheeks back to check its teeth. Nothing. I let out a huge sigh of relief and ruffled its ears, noticing for the first time that the dog wasn't an 'it' but was in fact a 'he.'

'You're a bad boy', I told him, stroking his sleek back coat.

I quickly realised that this was, of course, Des's dog. He'd never come inside our grounds before, but then I'd been pretty good at keeping the gates shut until now. I was about to get up and lead the dog safely back to my neighbour's house when my eyes were drawn to the black and white cat as it leapt from the wall and ran around the pond, launching itself into the hole. The dog remained sat and docile as I got up and shuffled as quickly as I could to the edge of the grave. I couldn't believe what I saw; the dog had obviously dug in the mud but had only found the rope attached to Danny's left wrist, pulling on it like a chew toy, wrenching my brother's fingers and palm through the surface. And now the cat was licking the rapidly decaying flesh, even using its paw to scoop some into its mouth.

'No', I screamed and the cat looked up at me, startled.

I flapped my arms at it and it responded by jumping up out of the hole and scooting through my legs up towards the house. The dog spotted it and with a high pitched bark, gave chase. Although the dog was more powerfully built, the cat was incredibly agile and skirted from side to side, keeping the Labrador at a safe distance. Like a fool, I tried to join in the chase and was soon on the path along the side of the house, a stiff legged jog taking me onto the front driveway. The dog seemed to have cornered the cat in front of the garage. I slowed to a walk, breath coming in short, ragged spurts, lungs burning, with the intention of stepping around the dog and trying to grab the cat myself. The little feline had other ideas as it first pounced to its right, making both myself and the Labrador move in that direction, and then, having wrong footed us both, it sprung to its left and towards the gates. I flicked out my right leg, hoping to bring it down but only managing to destabilise myself and bring the ground rushing up towards me for the second time in minutes. I lay facing the gate as the cat sprinted out into the road and the silver car appeared from the right. I heard the thud as it made contact with the cat and then the screech of tyres as the driver slammed on the brakes. As I stumbled to my feet and the Labrador made its own exit, charging out of the gates towards his home. The smell of burning rubber filled the air as I walked through the gates. I had a brief flashback to the blue car that had stopped at our gates during the infestation and how two of the occupants had ended up as mush on the tarmac. The car, a silver Ford, had safely come to a halt just before the end of my boundary wall. The driver had already pushed the button to put on the hazard warning lights and was getting out of his car, but talking to the people inside, a single index finger being raised in a clear indication that everyone else was to stay inside. The cat lay on the other side of the road. It looked crumpled and broken. The man, tall and wearing blue jeans, a white shirt and a brown, casual sports jacket started to walk towards it, arms out and palms up as he saw me.

'I'm sorry. I didn't see it, it just…'

I hadn't taken my eyes of the prone feline. I hardly heard the words coming from the man's mouth. He'd done my job for me. I couldn't be sure there was any risk but I'd been intent upon making sure and now this man, this car…

The cat's rear flank began to twitch, the hairs all along its spine stood up on end like there was an electrical current being run through its body. The cat's front right paw extended fully out like it was stretching after a nap, and then, slowly and deliberately, it tilted its head back on its neck, opened its mouth and let out a loud and terrifying hiss, ejecting blood and spittle over the road in front of it. The man jumped a little, his floppy hair bouncing on top of his head, but continued to walk towards the animal.

'Don't go near it, get back…'

'Hey, it's okay. I must have only clipped it, stunned it, I guess', he stepped forward still, bending at the waist and reaching out a hand towards the cat.

The cat turned and hissed directly at him. It lashed out one of its paws, caught the outstretched hand with several sharp claws and then it bolted off into the woods and out of sight.

The man hardly reacted. He just gave his hand a quick look and then collapsed to the floor. A blonde haired woman opened the passenger door of the car, got out, and began running towards what I could only assume to be her husband. The faces of two children pressed against the back window of the car. She got halfway towards him when he sprang to his feet. I took an involuntary step backwards. He, as she froze in position, put his head back and roared, knees bent, arms reaching out for her, looking like a deranged surfer. He leapt at her, tackling her around the waist, taking her to the ground, ripping at her with fingers and teeth, her scream bubbling out of her torn throat. Her red coat had been pulled open, her dress rapidly becoming the same colour, as he fed on her. The yells of the children made him lift his head and he pounced up again and ran at the car, smashing his fist through the back window, the voices of the kids more real now they were no longer insulated by the glass. I came to my senses; I had to help the children.

'Hey!' I screamed, waving my arms up and down. 'Over here.'

And he pulled his arm out of the car, blood dripping from the elbow, his clothes torn and ragged. He licked a line of the red liquid off himself, smiled, and charged straight at me. I backed off behind the gates, gripped the one that was still open and swung it as hard as I could, with my back, shoulders and hands yelling at me for the further abuse I was giving them. More by luck, it connected directly with the man's forehead as he tried to get at me. As I turned and ran towards the front door the burning image in my head was not of the cat lashing out, not the man attacking the rest of the people in his car, but of the dull, dead grey eyes with which he had stared at me.

I sprinted as hard as I could and halfway to the front door diverted towards the path down the side of the house. I had retained enough sense to remember, at the last second, that the front door was locked. I glanced over my shoulder when I heard the thing pursuing me bellow in anger and jump in one single motion from the road to the top of the wall. If it hadn't been raining, it would have caught me there and then. But it had been and its feet whipped out from underneath it as it landed on the damp stone. It clipped the wall on the way down, the sports coat fanning out like a cape as he fell inside the boundary, landing on one foot, using the other knee for stability on the chippings. I tore my eyes away and rounded the corner, using my hands to help my own balance as I made it to the top of the steps safely. I heard its snarling coming fast as I slammed the back door closed, twisting the key in the lock just as its first impact shook the door in the frame. I had to get away from that thing, because there was no way I was going to be able to stop it, not like I had with the previous creatures. This one was different. It was quick, it was openly aggressive and there was an awareness of its surroundings that the dim, shambling zombies of twelve months ago had never shown. Even more concerning was the fact that this thing was targeting individuals while one of the traits of the previous creatures which had helped us to survive was that they were drawn to groups of people and didn't pick off the weak or isolated. I stuffed my mobile phone and wallet into my jogging bottoms. I wrapped my fist around my keys and pushed myself towards the front door as fast as my wrecked body would let me. I got halfway there and turned, headed back towards one of the kitchen drawers, the one place where any kind of rubbish would end up and I swiftly dug around until I found the business card I was looking for. Leaving the draw open, I raced back to the front door. Still the thumps came from the back door, and then a smash as what I could only assume to be a fist shattered through. I opened the front door, stepped outside and slammed it shut as more glass broke at the back of the house and scattered across the kitchen floor. With all the strength I could muster, I forced myself to speed-limp to the garage door, pulling it open. I unlocked the Range Rover and pulled myself up into the driver's seat, starting the ignition and engaging the clutch, shoving the gear stick into reverse. My lower back cramped up and I let out a yelp of pain, bit my lip and forced my legs to work. The vehicle shot out backwards and I had to jam the brakes on, but still clipped the rear bumper off the far wall. I swung the steering wheel to the right and accelerated hard, crashing through the gates, popping them off their hinges and they fell to the ground with a dead metallic clunk. I had to pump the brakes again before I crashed into the trees opposite. I needed to get to Usk, get to the police station and warn people. But what could I tell them? How could I possibly explain how this had happened? Everyone had accepted how it came about last time because, well, last time it was down to the bad guys.

But this time?

Before I drove off towards in the direction of Usk I glanced left. The woman's body was still on the floor, one knee raised off the ground, surrounded by blood, her dress and hair covered with goo and her mashed up remains. She had no face and I selfishly felt glad that she had been killed outright and not had the opportunity to change. But the children? I could see right into the car, through the broken window. The hazards continued to blink and the engine was still running. With my higher vantage point from the cabin of the Range Rover I could clearly see that there was no one in there. They must have run off, hidden, I hoped.

Or something much worse.

I had no time to ponder further because the front door of my house, my home, exploded outwards as the creature charged through it, elbow raised in front of its face. I put the car into first gear and pushed down as hard as I could on the accelerator as I raised the clutch. The Range Rover wheel spun for a couple of seconds and then gained traction and pulled away, with what had been a family man taking his wife and kids out for a Sunday afternoon racing behind me, desperate to catch me and feed on my flesh. He cleared the fallen gates in a single jump, landed smoothly and with teeth gnashing, with legs and arms pumping, one fist trailing blood, sprinted after me. It was only when I cleared the first couple of bends and reached the straight level with the garden centre did I finally feel that I had left him behind. I floored the accelerator and headed for Usk.

30.

A police car with two officers inside sped past me at the petrol station as I came into town, the lights flashing but without the siren switched on. I pulled up directly in front of the main door of the police station on the right hand side of the street and stalled the engine in my haste to exit the Range Rover, even leaving the keys in the ignition. I climbed down from the cabin, legs stiff, back tightening up with every second, pushed on the blue door and entered the station. The public room was small with a desk, two upright chairs and an area set aside for those waiting to be seen. The two cushioned, low seats had seen better days and the foam was pushing its way out of the orange material that was only just holding together. There were two doors in addition to the one that I had entered; there was one marked Private directly behind the desk and another marked W. C. in the far right hand corner of the room. I approached the desk and the single officer who was stood behind it. He was on the telephone, his face and bald head almost purple with anxiety, the overhead light shining off him like a beacon. His uniform looked immaculate except that he wore no tie or hat.

'Two constables are on the way, I've called for extra officers', he was explaining. 'I don't know what else to say… okay… Yes, I will. How many hurt? What? What? Are you still there?'

He held the receiver to his ear for a few more seconds then hung up, raising a palm to me, then picked the phone up again and punched a series of numbers. He slammed the phone back into its cradle with a curse.

'Sir, now is not a good time…'

'It's happened again', I said. I tried to keep my voice as solid as possible, to ensure that my tone defined the gravity of the situation. The telephone rang and despite the look of confusion on his face, the policeman picked up.

'Usk Police station. Calm down, I can't… look, move to somewhere quieter, I can't…'

He dropped the phone.

'This cannot be happening.'

'What..?' I began and then I stopped myself.

What was going on?

I knew what was going on.

The officer held himself up by placing his two hands onto the desk in front of him. He was no longer purple; he was ashen.

'Sir, return to your home', he looked up at me, scrutinised me. 'Sir, you of all people know the procedure. I don't mean to be rude but we have situations in Caerleon and at the prison. So yes, we know it's happened again.'

The prison? Oh no way, the cat. Had it been drawn there or just wandered in that direction? That must have been where the police car had been taking off for. And Caerleon? Could the children have got there so quickly? Yes, of course they did. Because these weren't the shuffling zombies of

before, of last time, they were something else
entirely.

'It's not the same.'

'Sir, as I have said, we are fully aware of the
situation. I have made the appropriate calls and
right now you are not helping me. Return to your
home.'

Sweat had formed on his forehead and was now
running down towards his nose. He had picked the
phone receiver up again and was studying a sheet of
paper lined with telephone numbers.

'They are not the same', I said firmly. 'They can
jump, they can run, Jesus Christ. One of them tried
to chase me, he killed his wife, it's not...'

The smash of metal on metal was clearly two
cars colliding. From the sounds of it, and by the
loud yelling of people from outside, I guessed that
the accident had occurred on or near the bridge.

'Sir, I have to deal with whatever had happened
out there. I am ordering you to go home.
Immediately!'

He stepped around the desk and I realised what a large, intimidating man he really was. He stepped past me and out through the front door, scanning left and right, and then, as I suspected, headed off at a jog towards the bridge. I followed him out, the noise of a car horn filling the air with an impenetrable wail, but even above that it was possible to hear screams, shouts, anger and fear. I picked up my pace, attempting to catch up with the officer, when I saw him pause briefly, withdraw a small cylindrical object from his belt and snap it out to his side. The baton extended and he ran forward, up the shallow incline towards the bridge, exactly opposite the hairdressers.'

'Back off, back off. Sir, step away from the car. Step away from the car or I will have to use force.'

I had almost caught up with him when I saw the two cars, one a red sports car, the other a family saloon, which had collided head on, just on the town side entrance to the bridge. The driver's door of the car facing towards me, the green saloon that would have been heading into Usk, was open. And the man who had chased me from my own house, the man who had been scratched by the cat, had pulled the driver, a young looking man, from his seat as far as he could with the seatbelt still attached. He was holding all of the unfortunate driver's limp weight in one hand, as he chewed ravenously on the exposed neck, blood spurting across the windscreen of both cars. All around me people ran but were not sure in which direction to go. Some wanted so badly to help the poor wretch whose body was being consumed in front of them, but they couldn't bring themselves. Others turned and fled. The police officer advanced toward the murderous scene, baton cocked behind his right shoulder, ready to swing it at the demon in front of him. As he passed the red car he bent his knees and looked inside, made a signal for the occupant to get out and run from the car and into the town. Then he raised himself to his full height, took another step forward and began to swing his arm. Effortlessly, the creature let the now clearly dead man drop and as the baton flew towards its face, over the top of the open car door, it simply caught the officer's wrist, the snap as it was broken by the power of the grip alone louder even than the ongoing blare of the horn. Still holding the officer, who had now dropped his baton, it drew him to its face and bit him, holding its teeth in the policeman's cheek for a few seconds, and then threw him to the floor. The creature put its head back and roared, raising its arms above its head, fists clenched in victory. I could not move. I was frozen to the spot, just like all of the other people around me. I was not terrified, although, like the rest of us stood there, I should have been. I was held stationary because I was guilty; I had caused this.

The driver of the red car was the first one to move. From where I was stood I was just able to see the door open and a woman with long, dark hair emerge and start to scramble away from her wrecked vehicle. She may have made it too had she not stumbled, falling against the back end of her vehicle. The creature jumped to the roof of the green car in a single movement, baring its teeth, and then sprang across to the top of the sports car, landing with perfect balance. It caught the woman's hair in its left hand. Placing its right hand onto the roof, it then began to swing her from side to side, her arms flailing like a child's doll, and I saw her glasses fly off towards the wall of the bridge. She screamed once but then the crazed zombie simply smashed her head against the car, silencing her. It continued to pummel her skull against the metal, howling as it did so. Someone, a man, ran forward from behind me, but he stopped suddenly, shoes losing their grip on the wet road and he fell onto his backside with a grunt. Another howl joined the first, then another and then more until the chorus of animal noises filled the air and completely drowned out the car's horn. I now saw why the brave man at my feet had halted his advance. More than ten men stood on the crest of the bridge, all wearing the green trousers and shirts of the prisoners from the jail.

All of them had blood dripping from, or smeared around, their mouths. The first creature, the man whose only mistake was to want to help an animal that had run into the path of his car, stopped and turned to face them. He seemed to look directly at the prisoner closest to him, a shorter male with a skinhead and massive shoulders and chest and a mouth sized chunk missing from his forearm. The new arrival raised an arm and growled, then lowered its hand, pointing to the floor right in front of him. The creature on top of the car shook its head, bearing its teeth and shaking the body of the seemingly unconscious but hopefully dead woman once more. The group of zombies howled as one again and the first creature jumped down off the roof, dragging the body towards them. It laid the woman on the floor just where the finger had pointed towards and backed off, almost cowering. The creature at the front of the group bent down so that I could no longer see it behind the green car. More of the human observers were fleeing, some shouting, some crying, most screaming in terror. And when the apparent leader of the new arrivals stood up again, it held the gore dripping corpse above its head, like a trophy, her bloody and crushed head sagging down, her hair flicking back and forth in the wind across the white face of the infected prisoner. Turning its back to where I was stood, it let out the loudest scream I had ever heard and launched the woman's body into the crowd of its cohorts, who fell on her with snarls and yelps. I couldn't believe what I was seeing. There was a group mentality within them. There was a hierarchy. There was no way we were going to survive this.

I still had not moved as the leader of the prisoners began to walk across the bridge. It was only when the police officer pulled himself up and joined in the parade of the dead that the spell was broken. I turned and ran towards the Range Rover as fast as I could push myself. I had gone only a few yards, felt I just about to get myself out of their line of sight when I heard a clipped noise, almost a bark, and realised that I had been spotted and that one of them had been dispatched to take care of me. I ran even harder, muscles screaming at me, but the Range Rover was only strides away. I got to the door and swung it open, leaping in with a single motion. As I slammed the door shut, clicking the manual lock into place I saw the police constable charging toward me. He, no it, rammed a shoulder into the back of the vehicle and I turned the key in the ignition. The engine sprang to life and I slipped it into first gear, pulling away before any more damage could be done. I didn't know where I was going but knew I had to get out of Usk. I followed the road around, past the King's Head and up towards the town square. As I approached Bridge Street again, this time with the intention of turning right and away from the zombies, people ran across my path. I jammed on the brakes to avoid hitting them but then three prison green clad creatures hurtled out of nowhere after them. I couldn't look, forced my self not to observe as the macabre chase continued. Glancing both ways as quickly as I could at the junction, I accelerated right and away from the square, towards the dual carriageway. Would I go north or south? It had to be south, towards Newport or Cardiff. There would be more people there, more possibilities of safety. As I passed Usk's last residential area, I thought of Nick. He lived only about eight hundred yards away, I could turn round and go and get him and the kids.

Oh, no. The children.

I slowed the Range Rover and pulled across to the right hand side of the road, preparing to swing all the way back around, when in my side view mirror I briefly glimpsed two shapes running straight at the car. I made the mistake of looking over my shoulder and realised one of them was Tommo. I was considering stopping, letting them in and driving them away when Tommo threw himself onto the bonnet, moving from sprawling to standing in a microsecond. The other one drove an elbow through the passenger door window and rammed his face through the broken glass, slicing his cheeks, his forehead and bellowing right into my face. The sound of the car horn on the bridge could once again be heard. I pushed the gear stick into reverse and floored the accelerator, flipping Tommo off the bonnet and onto the floor. Tommo's infected friend held firm, his teeth snapping at me. I braked as hard as I could and he finally released his grip, tumbling backwards away from me. I sped forward again, leaving Usk behind, Tommo and the other zombie were now on their feet and chasing after me, but I increased the gap between us until they finally slowed their pace. I watched in the mirror they stopped, looked at each other, and then ran back towards the town.

***

I was lucky it was Sunday. The dual carriageway was clear and I accelerated to over ninety miles an hour until I reached the first lay by. Not indicating, I pulled in and dug around in my jogging trousers until I found my mobile phone and the business card I had rescued from the kitchen draw. After first flicking the business card onto the passenger seat, I brought up Nick's number and hit the green button to call him. It rang through to his answer phone message, but I hit the red button and immediately called him a second time with the same outcome. I threw the phone onto the passenger seat in frustration, then snatched it up again and selected his house phone. I let it ring over twenty times before finally giving up. I scrambled through the glove box, pushed the binoculars out of the way and found a mobile phone charger. I plugged it into the car's cigarette lighter while turning on the radio, trawling the airwaves for a local station. I realised I had best not sit here for too long with the broken window being such an easy way for those creatures, those zombies, the infected, to get access to me. I realised I had made the right decision to drive south as every radio station told me the same thing; get to a city, get to the coast. There were no explanations, there was only panic, and in the ten minutes I was parked up in the lay by, I had to retune the radio over six times as, one by one, each station went off the air.

31.

Once the final radio station has cut its transmission I felt more isolated and lost than I had ever been before. I was nearing the M4 and had to make a vital decision; left and head for England over the Severn Bridge, right to take myself to Cardiff, or straight over and into Newport. The inside of the Range Rover was freezing cold despite having the heater turned on to its highest setting. The wind whistled in through the shattered window, the trees around me passed by in a green blur that came into slightly more focus as I slowed down and picked up my mobile phone once again. With the same hand I managed to snag the business card from the passenger seat and with a great deal of difficulty entered the handwritten number on the back of the card into my phone. I cast the card aside, the breeze forcing it down into the foot well of the empty passenger seat. I pressed call, not expecting to get an answer so was dumbstruck for a few seconds when the phone at the other end was picked up after just a couple of rings.

'Mitchell.'

I heard the voice, the name, but was unable to take in that I had actually gotten through.

'This is Captain Mitchell and if this is not an important call then please get off my line.'

'Captain Mitchell. It's me. It's Matt Hawkins.'

'What do you want?'

'I'm at the M4 by Newport. Where do I go? Where is safe?'

For the first time since I had left Usk, a car zipped past me, jammed full, overloaded with passengers.

Just static.

'What? I didn't hear you?'

'Cardiff. Get to Cardiff. If you can't get to the Bay then at least get to the Stadium.'

I was approaching the roundabout and I moved over to the right hand lane that would guide me towards Cardiff.

'The Millennium Stadium?'

That was the last place I thought he would have told me to go.

'Yes, it's safe there. The most secure building in the city. Good luck.'

He hung up. I guessed one desperate civilian was not the most important thing for him to have to deal with right now but at last a member of the services had done something that benefited me. I flipped the phone off and placed it back on the spare seat. I snatched it straight back up again and tried both Nick's mobile and home numbers. Still no reply. I did not want to think the worst, but Usk must have been totally devastated by now. The speed those things moved with was terrifying. And what had happened on the bridge, when the first zombie had presented that poor woman to the leader of the prisoner creatures? They were so different from the first infestation. What could have possibly caused that? Well, I had caused all of this, of course. The authorities had thought that every scrap of the previous epidemic had been destroyed. They had gone to every length possible to ensure that this was the case. It had been me who had stopped them from achieving this, by thinking I could save my brother and that I could somehow return him to the person, the brother that he had been. And in the end, even he had not wanted that. Leading me to have to bury him in our garden and then…

The cat? Was it as simple as that? That the toxin had affected the cat in a different way? That when the infection was passed back to humans, it had changed, mutated even? Or had it changed in Danny?

Because I had tried to… to tame him?

But the way they moved now, the speed, the ability to jump? It could only be as a result of toxin within Danny combining with the animal. As I pulled onto the motorway I slowed down and swung the Range Rover onto the hard shoulder. I had no right seeking safety. I had no right to live. This was my fault. Nick and his children were probably already dead because of what I did. I rested my head on the steering wheel and screamed as loud as I could.

**

I sat for about twenty minutes, gripping the steering wheel so tightly that my knuckles were white and my hands had started to ache. Several cars had gone past me in the direction I would soon be headed but more were going the other way. The engine was still idling and the fuel gauge was indicating that I still had three quarters of a tank of petrol left. That would be more than enough gas to get me to Cardiff. I relaxed my grip and dipped the clutch, engaged the car in first gear and glanced in my rear view mirror before pulling out into the slow lane. I accelerated and moved up through the gears and noticed that a B. M. W. was fast approaching from behind, the driver flashing the headlights. I slowed a little, letting it catch up with me. The aqua marine coloured sports car drew level with me, three people crammed into the front seats. The passenger lowered his window and began shouting across to me. I signalled to slow down a little until I could make out their words.

'Do you know where to go? Where's safe?'

The man's voice was just about audible over the noises of the two engines and the air whipping over the cars. I could see a blonde sat in the middle but couldn't make out the driver.

'Where are you going?' he shouted again.

'The Bay', I yelled. 'Or the Millennium Stadium.'

'What? Where?'

We were approaching a bridge that passed over the motorway. I glanced up and saw there were a group of about five people stood on it, seemingly watching our progress. With a quick scan from left to right it rapidly became apparent that they were trapped; hordes of zombies were massed on each end of the bridge. Suddenly two of the assemblage leapt from the bridge, followed by the other three. They landed in a still moving heap directly in front of us. I slammed on my brakes and was thrown forward into my seat belt as the Range Rover decelerated quickly, lucky that the brakes had not locked up into a skid. The occupants of the sports car had been focussing their attention on me and had not spotted what was going on ahead. The driver reacted extremely late and the car went into a slide, ploughing through the middle of the suicide jumpers, flattening at least three of them. The car then went into a spin, the front bumper impacting upon the central reservation, flipping it up into the air. It rolled twice and finished on its roof, throwing up bright orange sparks, making a noise not unlike finger nails down a chalk board before finally coming to rest about twenty yards past the bridge. The zombies leapt off the overpass as one. There were twenty, thirty, maybe even forty of them. They kept pouring over the edge like an averlanche. Mostly, they landed with ease but a few slipped in the blood that covered the motorway. The B. M. W. had dragged one of the bodies with it as it had careered towards the barrier, leaving a long streak of red gunk along the floor. The creatures tore at the flesh of the dead and injured spread across the motorway. I ducked low behind the steering wheel, hoping they wouldn't become aware of my presence. Suddenly screaming filled the air. I raised my head just enough so I could see the stricken sports car. The blonde woman, face covered in blood, was dragging herself from out of the shattered front wind screen. I couldn't see if she was the only survivor but she was still in huge danger. Could I get to her in time? I sat upright but before I had chance to move forward, one of the zombies, a male, stood upright from its feeding frenzy. Unbelievably, it was wearing a white, towelling dressing gown and nothing else. Apart from the fact that it was drenched in blood, I could not see any marks or injuries. It let out a roar and pointed a single index finger towards the woman as she continued to crawl away from the car in the opposite direction to the creatures. As soon as the roar ended, two other zombies leapt up to their feet, faces still wet with blood and flesh, heads twitching from side to side, and sprinted towards the woman.

I couldn't help myself. They'd not realised I was there. I was sure that I could have slipped away, reversing back up the motorway. No other cars had come along in either direction. But I could not just sit there and do nothing. I screamed as loud as I could;

'RUN!'

As one, the zombies froze and they all turned towards the Range Rover.

'Oh...'

I jammed the gear stick into first and accelerated towards them. I adjusted my direction slightly to aim for the least dense section of the creatures, but even so, the Range Rover rocked as I hammered through their already decaying bodies, some bouncing off the front bumper but, surprisingly, most of them stepped or jumped out of the way at the last moment. And in a second I was clear of them, bringing the car to the left of the motorway to avoid the wreck of the smashed B. M. W. I slowed momentarily to see if it was worth trying to help the woman who had survived the car crash.

What I saw repulsed and terrified me, actually making me jerk my foot covering the brake so that I almost came to a halt. The zombies had not torn her to pieces but had pinned her to the floor and had bitten her left bicep just once. She continued to wail and thrash in their arms, but there were two of them and they were far stronger than she would have been even without her injuries. The fought with all of her heart until she collapsed to the floor for a moment and when she looked up again, her eyes had changed. They were turning people into their kind on purpose. They understood how the infection worked and how to make more of us like them. How could they..?

Suddenly there was the blare of a horn from behind me and a bus appeared out of nowhere, ploughing into and crushing the three infected people, the two zombies and the woman they had bitten, before disappearing down the motorway away from me. I looked in my mirror and saw that whoever the driver was had picked his spot right through the middle of the zombies that had charged at me. Bodies were strewn all over the motorway, some even thrown onto the opposite carriageway. Not all had been hit or fatally wounded and those left standing or hauling themselves to their feet now spotted me and began to make their way towards the Range Rover. Some were running, some were limping, but their battered bodies not prepared to give up and fall to the ground, not while there was still food to be snared.

In seconds, they were left hundreds of yards behind me and I continued to press my right foot down on the pedal until I saw the motorway sign telling me I was just nine miles from Cardiff. There were more cars joining from each junction, but it was no busier than a regular Sunday, and I was able to pick my lane safely to take me towards Cardiff Bay. As I came off the motorway and eased up the slip road to the roundabout I was horrified. The exit I needed was blocked by a bus on its side. The back end of the vehicle was on fire, the flames licking the company logo from the metal panels. It was the same bus that had sped past me. The driver had obviously tried to take the turning too quickly and had lost control. Thick, black smoke spewed up into the air from the rear of the bus, I had no chance to make a decision about stopping and trying to help any survivors; three zombies were already in the wreckage, searching for human remains, looking for food. Despite the smoke, they must already have picked up on the scent of their prey as they didn't even turn their heads in my direction. I followed the roundabout around to the next exit and rejoined the road I'd just pulled off, a car pulling over so I could safely negotiate the junction. I was going to have to head for the Millennium Stadium.

32.

I came off at the next junction and followed the roundabout to the left, picking up the route towards the city centre. I was surprised by how quiet the roads were but drove steadily and carefully, always unsure of what I may be faced with around every bend in the road. One thing was for certain; they'd gotten here before I had. Along the route, several cars had been abandoned, some with their doors still open. There were bodies in the gutters, on the pavements, in the middle of the road. Worse were the pools of blood with no evidence of the corpse that caused them, except for drops or trails of blood that emanated away from them. Either the zombies were fully consuming their prey or were carrying out the same action that I saw on the motorway and were turning more and more of us into them. I shuddered in my seat, the muscles in my back shouting out their objection. Looking down the side roads, I glimpsed the occasional movement but made no effort to turn or stop to check for any survivors. It was far more likely that what I was seeing were the predators themselves, either hunting down any people still out on the streets or trying to find a way into the houses, flats and shops. I came to the top of a rise, knowing that when I dropped down I had to bear right and drive alongside the castle wall. I would be trapped in a bit of a gully with walls on both sides for about four hundred metres, so I slowed down and pulled the Range Rover across the road to give me a direct view of the clear route ahead.

I was about to accelerate again when I noticed an arm waving at me from the recessed doorway of a house just up ahead. A head bobbed out and back in again, and then the action changed from a wave to a beckoning action. Was it someone in need of help or had the creatures become even more aware? I edged forward, until I was able to see more of the person in the doorway. It was a man and there was no way he was a zombie. I swung across so the passenger door was right in front of him.

'Get in, quick.'

He stepped out of his small shelter and opened the door, slipping slightly as he tried to step up and inside. He wore jeans and a black puffer jacket, rimless glasses and a blue baseball cap. He slipped and nearly fell into the gutter.

'Bloody hell' he shouted, rubbing his left knee from where he had bashed it on the frame of the Range Rover.

'Just get in!'

But we had already given our position away. Fast movement on my right caught my attention and I turned my head to see a woman running right at me, shrieking with her mouth wide open, front teeth exposed. Half her face was missing and her eye drooled out of its socket, bouncing against her exposed cheekbone as she ran. The right side of her body was covered in blood and I instinctively reached over the passenger seat and grabbed the man by his coat, lifting my foot off the clutch in the same movement. The Range Rover leapt forward and she clattered into the rear wing, her hands slapping along the bodywork trying to gain purchase. I watched in the mirror as she lost balance and hit the floor hard, sliding along the tarmac before, in a single motion, she was back on her feet and chasing after us. I was going no more than ten miles an hour but the passenger door was still wide open and the new travelling companion's legs remained dangling outside.

'Pull yourself in', I bellowed, aware that we now had walls on either side of us and that if he fell there was nowhere for him to run to. Luckily the road was straight and I was able to tug at his jacket again until he finally swung his feet inside just before the passenger door struck a lamp post and slammed shut.

'Bugger, bugger, bugger.'

'Are you okay? Are you bitten?'

'Bugger, bugger, bugger.'

312

I hit him across the side of his head with the flat of my palm, knocking his cap off, showing his curly black hair.

'Are you bitten?'

'No, no. I'm just terrified, so get off me.'

'If you'd rather get out here, that's fine with me.'

The Castle was now on our immediate right and I could see the corner of it ahead, where I would have to turn to the right and follow the wall around.

'I'm sorry, I'm sorry. It's just… What the hell is going on? They killed my Mum!'

He started to cry, banging his hands on the dashboard in front of him. I realised for the first time that this was no man but a teenage boy. He was tall but could be no more than seventeen.

'Why are you going this way? You need to get out of town This is where they've all been heading for.'

And the signs of it were all over the place. Bodies, blood and more of the zombies themselves.

They turned their heads as we passed but none tried to intercept us like the woman had done, but, then, we'd been static when she started her attack. Had they worked out that a moving car was a danger for them? This was unbelievable.

'Listen, I've been told by the Army to get to the Stadium. It's meant to be safe. So that's where I'm going. Like I said', I turned right, the Castle's main entrance now visible, 'That's where I'm going. And if you don't like it, take your chances with them!' I pointed at a group of zombies, all shirtless, who had surrounded three men against the Castle walls.

'No chance.'

That finally shut him up.

Two police cars passed us going the other way, without their lights or sirens on. Occupants of both cars were signalling that we should be going in the other direction. The kid turned in his chair, watching the cars as they sped away and looked at me, arms raised in a questioning shrug.

314

'I know what I've been told,' I shouted, the panic rising from my stomach to my throat and turned left at the Angel Hotel. Halfway through the turn I slammed the brakes on. The kid slipped forward and braced himself with the flats of his hands against the dash.

'Oh my God', he said, looking to his right, out of my side window and across the bridge at the sight that had stopped me, and the Range Rover, in our tracks.

Walking across the bridge were hundreds of zombies. Even from this distance it was possible to see that their lips had peeled back with the end result of making their teeth look more pronounced. Some limped but most walked as they had before they became infected and then, when they saw us, they screamed and they ran. I put my foot as hard down on the gas as possible and the Range Rover accelerated down the tree lined avenue. Cars were parked tightly on each side of the road but there was no sign of any people or any more of those creatures. As we approached the entrance to the old Cardiff Arms Park rugby ground and one of the main entrances to the Millennium Stadium a group of soldiers stepped out into the road and trained their weapons directly at us. I braked hard again, the boy next to me this time placing his feet up in front of him to stop him from sliding forward, raising his arms in the air with the universal sign of surrender.

'We're human, we're human,' he shouted.

We had partially slid to a halt just in front of the soldiers. They wore full battle gear including helmets and body armour. The lead officer pulled my door open before I had chance to react.

'Pull forward to the bottom of the ramp. To that space there, leave the keys in the ignition and run, and I mean run, up to the turnstiles. You'll be told what to do next. Go.'

'Wait', I shouted as he slammed the door. 'They're coming from that way.'

'You think we don't know that? They're coming from everywhere. Now move!'

I brought the Range Rover forward to where another solider directed me as I pulled in to the final space in a row of cars, completing a make shift barrier, and turned off the ignition. It was only when I got out did I realise what was going on directly in front of me. A row of cars had been parked across the road and ten, maybe twelve soldiers were firing in sustained bursts over the top of the bonnets as dozens of zombies charged at them. Then from behind me, the first shots were fired towards the creatures we had seen coming over the bridge. Grabbing the teenager by his jacket, I sprinted up the slope towards the stadium entrance without looking back. The sound of shots, screams, bellows and wails chased behind us, pushing us on to even more effort. By the time we reached the turnstiles my lower back and the tops of my legs were cramping up and I stumbled. The kid let me fall, left me lying there and ran towards the soldiers. They let him through the barriers and then he was gone out of my sight.

'Get up, move it', shouted a trooper as he ran towards me, grabbing me under one armpit, pulling me to my feet. Once through the first set of gates, he pointed me in the direction of one of the huge steel doorways.

'In there, and do exactly as you're told.'

I dashed through the doorway into the concrete causeway that encircled the inside of the Stadium. Through the entrance to the stands I could see hundreds of people already inside, some on the seats and some on the pitch itself. There were dozens more soldiers between me and there though and without a word I was ushered into the nearest men's toilets. I moved without a sound but kept my hands raised because the two soldiers who directed me had their guns aimed at me. There were three more armed soldiers in the toilet.

'We need to check you haven't been infected. Take off your clothes.'

I did as directed, realising that the jogging trousers and sweatshirt were damp with perspiration. I laid my wallet and mobile phone on top of a pile of boxes and military equipment positioned in the middle of the floor. I was surprised that I hadn't left them in the car.

'Clear', shouted someone.

'Turn around.'

'Clear.'

'Okay, put your clothes back on. Where have you come from and have you had any run-ins with those things?'

'Usk. I'm from Usk', I said as I dressed myself, pleased not only to be clothed but also that there were no longer guns aimed right at me. 'The town was being torn to pieces. I've been chased but no direct contact.'

'Okay. Go through to the pitch side. We may want to speak to you again about what you've seen, so don't go too far.'

'Sure.'

I stuffed my wallet back into my trouser pocket but kept my phone out and brought up Nick's mobile number. I pressed call, expecting nothing, but as I walked through and took a seat in the bowl of the stadium, Nick answered.

'Matt', he whispered. 'You've got to help us.'

'Nick! Nick! Oh no. Where are you?'

'Keep your voice down. We're in the loft. I turned it into a safe room. We've got food and water but those things… they're looking for us. It's like they can smell us.'

' Nick, I…' There was a bang from Nick's end of the line.

'Shhh.' Then nothing for over ten seconds. My head went back and I saw for the first time that the roof was closed over. No wonder Mitchell had been so convinced that this place was safe.

'One of them was on the roof. Please come and help us, please…' and the line went dead. I shook my mobile phone, not quite sure what I was expecting to happen. I called Nick's phone again but got nothing. I looked at my phone's screen and saw my signal had gone.

'No.'

There was a sudden burst of sustained gun fire from the door way behind me followed by heavy footsteps, and then voices.

'Drop back, drop back.'

More gun fire, a yelp of pain and then screams.

'Close the door, close the door now.'

'But, Sir?'

'Close the door now! That's an order.'

Gun fire again and I jumped to my feet and turned to face the exit when, mixed in with the shots, came the unmistakeable growl of the zombies as they charged at the Stadium. The metal door slammed into place, the noise echoing around the concrete corridor, muting the continued gun fire outside.

From where I was stood I could not see the main door, but now a few soldiers came into my line of vision. Even though the door was closed, they still trained their weapons in that direction as the metal was pummelled with what I could only assume to be the fists of the dead outside.

'It'll hold', said the authoritative voice that had demanded the doors be closed in the first place.

And then, from a seemingly younger soldier, the worst words possible;

'Sir, I've been bitten.'

The troops that I could see backed off. A couple of them dropping into firing position and they raised the sights of their guns up to eye level. The hammering at the door continued. More people crowded around where I was stood.

'Oh please, please', and then a louder 'No!'

'I'm sorry, son.'

The echo of the discharged bullet rang around the stadium. Everyone, soldiers and civilians alike, either flinched or stepped backwards. Some of the troops turned their back on the scene. Others leant their guns against the nearest wall and stepped out of sight, then reappeared, dragging the body of their fallen comrade across the grey floor past the toilet where I had been checked for injuries. The officer in charge, the one who had pulled the trigger on the final shot, walked around the corner and towards us. He was a short and squat man with thick forearms. Like the rest he wore standard Army camouflage gear and a peaked hat that didn't quite cover a scar that ran along his forehead.

'Please get back from the doors. Find somewhere and settle yourselves in. Now!'

People, myself included, did as we were told immediately.

33.

There must have been at least three thousand people within the lower sections of the Stadium. Some were alone, others had grouped together. Only the occasional soldier prowled the upper levels. My stomach groaned and I realised I had not eaten. I was surprised I did not feel worse after the amount I had drunk the previous day but I guessed that adrenaline was coursing through my body, getting rid of all kinds of ills, except for the pain in my lower back. The muscles were still tight but they had not gone into spasm again and I counted that as a huge bonus at this point. I thought about Nick and the children, locked in their own attic, hoping that the zombies would move on, that they wouldn't be discovered. How much food did they have? How frightened were the kids? What could I do to help? I sat more upright in my chair. What the heck was I doing sat here when I could be helping them? I could get to the Range Rover and get back to Usk.

The journey between here and there would be relatively clear of incident. The difficult part was going to be getting out of first the Stadium and then the city. I couldn't see that the soldiers were just going to roll the doors open for me to take off on my crusade while those creatures were trying to smash the door down to get to their next meal.

I got up off my seat and walked through to the concrete alleyway. From the landing above I could hear irregular gunfire, single shots as opposed to the continuous rounds of automatic weapons. I could see a lone soldier at the top of the stairs poised at a shattered window. He held a sniper rifle in his hands as he looked out, scanning the approach to the stadium. He would watch for a while, then aim the weapon and fire off a shot. I hoped that he was clearing the area around my car and would inadvertently help me in my quest. I just had to come up with a way to get out of the stadium.

I ducked inside the toilet, the same one where I had been forced to strip off my clothes to prove that

I had not been bitten, and turned on the tap. I closed my eyes and splashed water on my face. I leaned forward and let my forehead rest on the cold glass of the mirror. I could still hear the semi-regular crack of the rifle from the first floor landing. I placed my hands on the wall either side of the mirror and pushed my face away. I continued to study the reflection, but I wasn't looking at myself. I was looking at the pile of heavy hardware and boxes that I could see over my right shoulder. The same pile I had laid my clothes on top of. I let my eyes run down the mirror until I could see the floor around the bottom of the military equipment. It wasn't the same as the rest of the tiled area. I spun around and quickly dropped to my knees. It was a manhole.

Why had it been covered?

Because it clearly led somewhere outside of the stadium walls and if the zombies got into the sewers, then they might just find their way in. I wondered how many similar access points there were and if they'd all been covered over. The toilet I was in seemed like the one in most use so I would be stupid to try to shift the equipment here, but maybe there was another toilet, further along the corridor, that would allow for more privacy. I exited the toilet and instead of going left and back to my seat, I turned right, directly into the path of one of the soldiers.

'Access out here is limited. Go back inside to your seat.'

I didn't want to cause a scene or draw any more attention to myself so turned on my heels and went back inside to consider my options.

The banging on the roof started about ten minutes later. It was sporadic but it echoed around the stadium and drew everyone's attention. Watching those around me crane their necks towards the sound reminded me of the zombies outside the gate of our house in Usk when they looked up at the moon. A few people got to their feet, others pointed and the general hubbub of conversation grew until a number of people, men and women, gathered into a group and then began to walk towards me. I couldn't think what they expected me to do but I was mistaken; they bypassed me and went straight out into the corridor, shouting that the soldiers needed to start doing something. Two troops ran towards them, weapons drawn but pointed towards the floor.

'You need to go back inside. We're dealing with enough without…'

'They're on the roof…'

'What are we going to ..?'

'Help us…'

They spoke over him before he had a chance to explain and then the jostling started. I got to my feet and stood in the doorway. This could be just the distraction I needed. The lead soldier tried to stem the tide but one of the women was screaming right into his face and he pushed her away from him as his colleague called for back up. Pandemonium broke out as the woman fell to the floor, a cigarette lighter bouncing out of her pocket. I bent and picked it up immediately. One of the men shoved back at the soldier who reacted by bringing his gun up to firing position, shouting for everyone to back off. The rest of the group did so but more people came running from the pitch toward the melee. As the stand off intensified I took my chance. As more soldiers appeared from the corridor I stepped to the left, out of their way, with my hands raised to shoulder level to indicate that I didn't want any trouble. Despite the raised weapon, more pushing and shoving began and as the troop reinforcements intervened, I slipped away along the corridor. If I was spotted now all I would have to say was that I was getting out of the way, that I wanted no part of what was going on. If I wasn't, I would duck into the next toilets and see if there was a possibility of getting out through the drains.

The ladies' toilet had been turned into the morgue. In the corner, covered with a thin sheet, was the body of the solider that officer in charge had euthanized. There was no chance of that one coming back to attack anyone; the puddle of blood that had formed around the head was testimony to that. I'd been right about the manhole though; it was there, covered in a stack of heavy, robust green plastic boxes. It took me almost half an hour to re-stack them about a foot closer to the door, so they no longer blocked access to the metal plate. If anyone were to glance inside on a quick inspection, they would think that nothing had changed. I lifted the cover and placed it to one side. I peered down and saw that there was a ladder built into one side of the concrete wall. The narrow tunnel below had a walkway on either side of a stream of filthy looking water. I brought the plastic lighter I'd acquired from my trouser pocket and placed my left foot on the first rung of the ladder. In a few careful steps I was down on the narrow walkway. I flicked the lighter to life and looked about me. It was dark but I could make out enough that I'd be able to find my way around. I extinguished the flame and put the lighter back in my pocket beside mobile phone and placed one foot back onto the ladder, boosting myself up so I could quietly pull the cover into place above my head. I stepped back down and once again brought the tiny flame to life. I followed the passageway back under the way I'd come and shortly came to another set of steps that I confidently assumed led to the first toilets. I bypassed these and continued on until I reached the junction that I believed would take me out under the walls of the stadium and towards my car. My footsteps echoed dully around the narrow passageway. I fanned the light further on ahead and saw that there was a warren of passages running under and around the Stadium. Stepping with more care to ensure I made next to no noise I advanced towards what appeared to be a miniscule sliver of daylight permeating the darkness ahead. I found the steps built into the wall and followed their path upwards. The rusted underside of the metal cover was directly above my head. I mounted the steps and, having boosted myself up high enough to reach, pressed my left palm on the underside of the cover. The single gunshots had now become louder. No more regular, but definitely louder. I pushed upwards and the seal of the manhole popped slightly as it freed itself from its moorings. I looked around in a complete three hundred and sixty degree circle. I couldn't believe it. I had come out no more than five metres from the Range Rover. There were no zombies in the immediate area but I could see and hear them up at the entrance to the Stadium. To get to me before I made it to the car they would not only have to cover the distance but would also have to navigate the turnstiles. Checking my pockets for my few meagre possessions, I went for it.

I drove my legs upwards and the lid burst away from me. Using my arms as well as my lower extremities I powered out of the sewer, dropping to my knees immediately and put the manhole cover back into place. It made a dull but far too loud clunk as it slid back into its housing.

Big trouble!

I straightened up and saw two of the infected had seen me and were now running in my direction. I froze on the spot. There was no way I was going to be able to evade them. So this is how it was going to end. I had failed Danny. I was going to fail Nick and his children. And now I was going to die.

The two rapid gunshots brought the two zombies to the floor, their finally dead carcasses sliding to a halt just a yard from my toes, brains smeared across the floor behind them.

'MOVE.'

The shout had a dual effect. It got me on my toes toward the Range Rover but it also acted as a signal to the rest of the creatures to attack me. I tore the driver's door open and threw myself in. My back screamed in pain but I had to ignore it as I grabbed for the keys and, finding them, turned them in the ignition. The engine burst into life and I jammed the gear stick into reverse as the hungry screams closed in on me. The gunfire continued but although some of the zombies were struck and wobbled as they pursued me, very few headshots were actually made, so not many fell to the floor. Well, not as many as I would have liked, anyway.

Without closing the door I accelerated backwards and away from the macabre masses. When I had put some distance between myself and them I swung the steering wheel to the left and jabbed my foot down on the brake. The Range Rover pivoted across the road and in the first act of the fastest turn in the road I had ever made, my door slammed shut. I selected first gear, pulling the wheel in the opposite direction and drove as hard as I could away from the Stadium. I sped towards the castle, moving up through the gears and, more importantly, moving away from the chasing creatures. As I approached the junction I boxed the gears from fourth to second preparing to turn right, I looked in the mirror. There was no way they were going to catch me, no matter how hard they continued to charge. I raised the middle finger of

my left hand to them and accelerated away along
the deserted streets.

34.

I stopped in the middle of the road, straddling the white lines, about a hundred metres short of the 'Welcome to Usk' sign. I had phoned Nick as soon as I'd cleared an eerily quiet Cardiff. The relief in his voice that I was coming back for them and that there was a safe place to take his family made the hairs on the back of my neck tingle. He'd told me that there'd been no further footsteps on his roof and that he'd not heard any noise from outside in quite some time. I was unsure whether this was his mind playing tricks on him or Nick simply saying anything he could to guarantee that I would not back out. Either way I did not care. I may have failed my brother but I was not going to fail those children and their father. I dug into my trouser pocket and pulled out my mobile phone and brought up Nick's number. As I pressed the green call button I hoped that the network was still up and running. I finally breathed out when my ear was filled with the ringing tone.

'Matt?' answered Nick in less than a whisper.

'Yeah. I'm here. Anything?'

My eyes bounced all around me, double checking every movement, every blade of grass that blew in the breeze.

'Nothing. I swear. I'm not going to risk bringing the kids out if they were still out there.'

'Okay. I'll drive down your street. I'll beep twice as I pass, then I'll turn around at the end and pull up right outside your front door. I beep once and you come out. Any more than once and you get back upstairs.'

'Got it.'

'Get ready. I'm on my way.'

I pressed the red button and slipped the phone onto the passenger seat. My heart was trying to dig its way out of my chest with a series of explosions. I waited for a few seconds and realised that the only thing that was going to stop the fireworks inside my ribs was to pull my car back on the road towards Cardiff with Nick and his family inside. I slipped the Range Rover into first gear and pressed my right foot down on the accelerator.

Nick's street was clear. It held twelve detached houses on each side of the road, each with a driveway and a wide front lawn. At the end was a turning area which I was pleased to see was free of obstacles. Their house was the third on the right and as I drove past it I pumped the horn quickly, twice. I sped up, moving from second to third gear, swivelling my head from side to side until I braked, swinging the steering wheel to the right and coming to a stop, directly facing the final house on the street. As I reversed I thought I saw a brief movement in the front lounge window and I paused for a split second before re-engaging the forward gear, squinting into the darkness behind the glass. A face smashed against the window, leaving a smear of blood. And then its eyes locked me in its dead, hungry stare and the thumping of my heart stopped for the two seconds it took me to get the heck out of there. I raced towards Nick's front door, sure I heard glass shattering behind me. I swung left off the road, across his neighbours garden and I hit the horn, one short but powerful blare, before I applied the brakes.

The front door burst open and Nick's face was right there, through the broken glass of the passenger window. I glanced up at my rear view mirror and slammed the car once again into reverse.

'NO!' screamed Nick.

I pushed my foot down on the gas pedal as far as it would go and released the clutch so the Range Rover shot backwards. The rear bumper smashed into the mid section of the zombie that had been running towards me. I heard a crunch, felt the Range Rover lurch with the impact and then I saw, in the mirror, the creature hit the deck and slide. I braked again but was primed and ready to run it down and crush the life out of it. I watched as the monster tried to get up but its shattered legs would not hold its weight. Instead it began, slowly, to drag itself in my direction. I knew it was moving too slowly to catch us.

Now I knew it was safe to collect Nick and the children. I pulled up to their door. Nick's mouth was still wide open so I made an arm cranking action, encouraging him to hurry up, to get the kids in the car. Robbie snapped his father out of his fugue by pulling open the back door and ushering the girls in, slamming the door once he had clambered in after them.

'Nick', I implored at the same time.

He shook his head and blinked, finally getting in beside me. Without a word he wrapped his arms around my shoulders.

'Matt, I… I…'

'It's okay. Nick. It's…'

'It's not okay', said Robbie, leaning forward between the front seats, pointing towards the end of the road. 'Look!'

I raised my eyes and felt my shoulders slump. Stood in the middle of the road, blocking our exit, was the zombie that had taken control on the bridge in Usk, the leader of the infected prisoners. He still wore the green trousers but had lost his shirt along the way. He was short but his shoulders, chest and arms were massive, muscular and defined. Blood had dried across his pectorals and had run down his face from a fresh gash on his bald head. The bite mark on his forearm was now simply a black, oozing hole. He returned Robbie's pointed finger, bore his teeth and let out a prehistoric roar.

'This guy is getting on my nerves', I said. 'Buckle up.'

The Range Rover bolted forward and I veered the car to the left of the monster ahead. He bent his knees, preparing to throw himself towards the car and I could see that he was lining up me as his target, that he was going to leap at my side window as we passed him. An instant before he could react, I swung the car to the right, directly into him and I heard the headlight shatter as we ploughed through him. The front end of the Range Rover felt like I had driven into a brick wall and I almost lost control, the steering wheel spinning in my hands for a second until I pulled it back under control. Something bounced on the black bonnet and then the prisoner's head, detached at the neck, slid across the windscreen and up and over the roof. I hit the wipers and as the blood was washed away I watched in the mirror as the headless body twitched and finally died in the road.

35.

I drove across the flyover, weaving slowly to avoid the cars and trucks that had either been abandoned or had smashed into each other. There were no people. There were no strewn bodies. The children remained quiet in the back seat. Robbie occasionally leaned forward and pointed out something terrible, some evidence of carnage on the road side. The girls, Sally and Jayne, did not make a noise all of the way down to Cardiff but simply sat with their arms around each other. I'd hoped they would fall asleep, that they would not see the desolation all around them, but so far they had not. For the duration of the journey we had not seen another moving car, which was heart breaking, but we hadn't run into any zombies either which gave me hope that we could reach the stadium safely, that it may in fact remain a sanctuary.

Nick had briefly filled me in on what had happened. After the first epidemic he had become worried that he had not done enough to protect his family. After Jenny left, he developed a deep rooted paranoia. He had sound proofed the attic, providing it with its own electricity source and a store of food. As soon as he'd heard the undead start to attack his neighbours, he had evacuated the family upstairs and despite a clear awareness from the creatures that fresh meat was close by, they had remained undiscovered. He'd fallen silent after a while and it played on my mind that he was running through the last time we had been together and the fact that he'd punched me. If he mentioned it, I had every intention of telling him I deserved it and that we were never to speak of it again. The road ahead was clearing and I was preparing to increase our speed when Nick, from his seemingly comatose state suddenly yelled out.

'Stop.'

I jammed on the brakes and was happy that the children were properly belted in. Nick was out of the Range Rover in a second, crossing in front of the bonnet and running over to the railings on my side of the flyover. Both girls let out a little whine and Robbie immediately began fiddling with the release button on his safety belt so he could follow his father.

'Robbie, no', I said softly, turning to face the children. 'You stay here and look after the girls, okay?'

He nodded bravely but his eyes told me that he was more filled with fear than at any other time in his short life.

'Nice one, buddy', I said as I opened my door and slid from the seat.

I left the engine running.

'Nick', I called in nothing more than a whisper. 'What are you playing at?'

'Look', he replied, pointing off at right angles to the direction our vehicle was facing.

I walked over to where he stood, my eyes everywhere all at once. I looked where he was pointing, along the road that ran beneath the flyover we had stopped on. It was a four lane dual carriage way that, about half a mile away, opened up into a shopping complex. The building at the front was a massive superstore and in its car park hundreds of people were massed.

'Look', Nick said again, finally lowering his finger. 'Maybe we don't need to go to the Stadium. It looks safe over there.'

I rested my elbows on the top rail and squinted off into the distance. Nick was right. There were hundreds of people over there, but something didn't seem right. It appeared that two huge queues had formed, one leading into the store and one leading away. It was just too far out of sight for us to make out properly what was going on.

'Wait a second', I said, surprising myself as much as Nick.

I ran back to the car and climbed across my seat, popping open the glove box.

'Is everything okay, Matt?' Robbie asked. He had positioned himself between his two sisters and held their hands in his.

'Everything's fine', I smiled, snagging the binoculars and running back to Nick.

I trained the lenses on the car park, scanned from left to right, and then felt as if all of my energy had seeped from my body.

'No', I breathed, and passed the binoculars to Nick.

He took longer than me, surveying from side to side, up and down. I knew the outcome would be the same and he slumped to the floor, his back against the railings.

'It's over, isn't it?' he asked.

I took the binoculars from him and shook my head.

'It's not over until those guys are safe', I said, gesturing towards the car.

But inside I knew Nick was right. What we had both seen across in that car park told us more about what was happening and how things were going to end than anything else we had previously seen. I didn't want to look but I could not help myself.

The entire car park was surrounded by zombies. There were hundreds of them, five deep, creating an inhuman fence. They had a tidal life as they rocked back and forth in unison. Nothing was getting in or out of their cordon. Two lines of unharmed humans were organised within the perimeter. One was made up of women, children and the elderly and they were being funnelled towards the entrance of the supermarket. The other line held just men, and they were being herded around the corner, out of our site. I remembered how the zombies had pinned down the woman from the crashed car on the motorway and how they had bitten her to convert her to one of their own. Dozens of zombies milled around across the car park, maintaining order with snapping teeth and snarls. Slowly the line of humans being taken inside thinned and then was gone as the last one was forced inside. I couldn't hear the crying but I had seen one child, a young girl, as she was shoved to the floor, her mouth blubbering as the woman with her tried to pull her to her feet. I watched as the zombies set a guard on the door and those not needed began to head towards the line of men.

'What are they doing?' asked Nick.

'They've put most of the people inside the shop', I replied.

'Why? Why would they do that?'

The answer was out of my mouth before I had time to check it.

'Where do we go for our food, Nick?'

He let out an anguished moan and Robbie called out to his father from the car.

'It's okay', Nick responded. 'We'll be on our way in a second.'

Nick climbed to his feet and took the binoculars from me. A second later he handed them back, and with a shake of his head, walked back to the Range Rover. I brought the glasses back up to the bridge of my nose and watched as the zombie perimeter began to close in around the men, slowly but surely boxing them in tightly. The humans started turning in circles, looking, searching and praying for a way out. One of the infected stepped forward and bit a tall, blonde man on the shoulder. I heard him scream. I watched him fall to his knees. Some of the others went to him and then backed off as he rose to his feet, already changed. I'd been right. Feeding time was inside but out here they were swelling their ranks. I watched it all. It seemed like it was slow motion as the first of the men threw a punch, and then another and more joined in and although the zombies were knocked to the ground, one, two, three more were always there to replace it. The men fought hard but as each of their side fell, then another joined the undead masses. I thought I had been watching for minutes but it was mere seconds and it was evident that the creatures were organised, that they knew not just what they wanted to achieve but how to do it.

'Matt', Nick called. 'Please, we've seen enough.'

And then someone broke free. He punched a zombie and the beast fell over, knocking several of the unbalanced undead to the floor. A group of the men, no more than ten of them, leapt through the space that had been created and sprinted away along the road. I tracked their path, thinking about how I could get our vehicle ahead of them and assist their escape. I had all of five seconds to consider this course of action before they were each cut down. The infected were not only fast and powerful but were also getting smart. As the men ran, stealing looks over their shoulders at their pursuers, another gang of zombies stepped into the road ahead of them. I watched as the first one was taken to the ground and realised that for these men there was going to be no second life. The binoculars shook in my hand as they tore his head from his neck and then the binoculars fell to the floor and cracked but

I did not care. Unless we got to the stadium, there was no hope for us.

***

I no longer drove with caution. There may not have been a single creature on the streets but that was not to say they were not there. They had gotten clever. They could have set all kinds of traps and as I piloted the Range Rover around the walls of Cardiff Castle I had already made up my mind that speed was our best option. Nick was silent, the girls were weeping and all I could hear, even over the whine of the engine, was Robbie telling his sisters that everything was going to be okay, that Matt was going to save them. I only hoped I could. Since the flyover my only thought had been of Danny, how I had failed to save him, and that now I had another chance and that I would die before I let this family be harmed. I slowed, getting ready to swing the car to the left, knowing it was only a few hundred metres to the manhole cover and the safety of the stadium. I changed down from third gear to second, touched the brake once more, gripped the steering wheel a little tighter and then the police car sped around the corner on the wrong side of the road, smashing into the front of the Range Rover and bringing both cars to a dead halt.

36.

I don't know how long I sat there with my chin on my chest but when I opened my eyes and the world around me swam back into focus it was through the shattered front windscreen of the Range Rover that I could see the broken remains of the police car. Its horn was blaring, jammed on, and I could see the driver slumped over the steering wheel. I considered trying to re-start our car, to reverse and get us out of there but steam hissed front the engine and the front suspension must have snapped as it sat sagged forward. I felt a sticky sensation on my chin which I gently probed with my finger tips and when I brought them up to my eyes they were smeared with blood. My clothes were drenched in it; the airbag had not deployed and my nose had impacted with the steering wheel. I ran my hand along the bridge of my nose and could feel the crack as well as the laceration. I unbuckled my seat belt and slumped forward. Nick was breathing heavily in the passenger seat next to me. I turned my head to him.

'Are you okay?' I asked.

He looked okay, but when he turned to face me I could see that the left hand side of his face was plastered in blood and that he continued to bleed from his ear.

'I'm…' he began. 'The kids!'

We both turned at once. Robbie, Jayne and Sally were sat stock still, their eyes wide and staring. I could see no blood and let out a sigh of relief. They had all kept their seatbelts on so had been protected from the impact. The boot of the car had popped open and a breeze blew through into my face. A slap on the window to my side of the car drew my attention and with a short scream I turned to face the infected man who pawed at me through the glass. His head turned from side to side, his tongue flicking across his blood encrusted lips. His hand continued to play across the window, leaving a thick, red trail. His dark grey eyes met my own and

I felt a part of my soul die. Slowly he brought his hand down the window and then he smiled at me. I suddenly realised he was moving his claw towards the door handle. I swivelled in my chair and as he pulled I kicked the door as hard as I could, to send the zombie tumbling backwards onto the road. The children shrieked as one and I reached out and snagged the door, pulling it back closed with a heavy thump. Before I had chance to snap the lock down both of the back doors of the Range Rover were wrenched open. Hands, decaying, wretched hands stretched in towards the girls. Sally yelled, Jayne was struck dumb. The rancid fingers wrapped themselves around their wrists, through their hair and after a brief moment of hope when their legs snagged in their seatbelts, they were gone.

'NO!'

Nick shouted and was out of the car in a moment. As soon as his feet touched the floor something hit him in the midriff and he was carried off to my right and crashed across the bonnet of the police car, wrapped up with a huge zombie specimen. The noise of crumpled metal filled the air and I knew I had less than no time to react. I twisted in my seat so I was facing the back of the Range Rover and I stepped over the gear stick and handbrake, flicking loose Robbie's seatbelt and bundling him into my arms. He was frozen, his eyes and mouth wide. I struggled over the back seats and out of the car via the wide hatchback. I jumped to the floor and the extra weight in my arms made me stumble forward, dropping Robbie into the gutter. I glanced over my shoulder. Over a dozen of the infected were descending upon our position. The girls and the zombies that had taken them were nowhere to be seen and Nick continued to struggle with his assailant. For a moment I considered rushing to his aid and then a geyser of blood spurted up from his neck as the infected being finally claimed victory. I picked Robbie up again and ran as fast as I could. It was then that I realised I was charging in the wrong direction, that I was taking Robbie away from safety, away from the stadium.

The castle wall was on my left and I stayed in as close to the shops on the opposite side of the road as I could, hoping that it would be less likely that I would be spotted. As I ran, leaving a trail of blood along the pavement, I saw that one of the shop doors up ahead was open, so I slowed slightly with the intention of jinking inside. What I saw in the doorway brought me to a complete halt; the remains of a woman wedged the door open. One of her legs was missing and her ribs had been peeled open, revealing a bloody cavern where her organs should have been. Her face was virtually untouched but her nose had been snipped off with what I could only assume to have been a single bite. Covering Robbie's eyes, I stepped over the corpse and glanced back out into the street. One of the zombies was running a finger along the ground near my vehicle. It brought the digit first up to its nose and then into its mouth. It was like a blood hound being given a fresh scent to follow. I ducked my head back inside the building as it looked my way but could not resist peering back out. It was male and stood in the middle of the street, the denim jeans it wore filthy and bloody. It had no shirt or shoes. And then it sniffed the air and stared along the road, looking directly at me. It pointed at me and I stepped out of its sight.

I pulled Robbie closer to me, trying to muffle his sobs against my chest.

'It's okay. I'm not going to let anything happen to you.'

'Dad! Dad!' he cried. 'My sisters.'

I turned around and realised for the first time that we were in a huge pub. The bar ran along the left hand wall with the rest of the area taken up by seating booths and tables with the chairs stacked on top. What was a pub doing open this early in the morning? I looked back at the dead woman in the doorway and realised that she must have been the early morning cleaner. Her mop bucket lay on its side just to the side of the door. A shadow fell over her prone body and I flinched as a lone zombie launched itself onto her, devouring what was left of her face in ravenous gulps. I had been frozen to the spot, but now I quickly and quietly moved behind the bar and ducked low. I could hear more footsteps, louder even than the feeding frenzy taking place one the floor, as another one entered the bar and paced around, sniffing the air trying to pick up on our scent. My nose had stopped bleeding but I was still covered in blood and that must have been like a beacon for the zombies. I held my palm over Robbie's mouth and placed a finger to my lips. His body was shaking but he tried his best to nod his head. There was a single, open door behind the bar and I decided that once the zombie had advanced far enough into the pub that we would make a break for it. I glanced around looking for some sort of weapon but apart from empty, clean beer glasses, there was nothing. I briefly considered trying to get to the overturned bucket and use the mop itself against the creature. It was a gamble that I decided was one step too far, especially considering the speed I had seen those things move. I could not arm myself and still make sure Robbie was protected. From the far end of the bar there came a crash as, I assumed, the zombie knocked some chairs from a table and I took that as our cue to go. I sprang to my feet and ran through the door, shoving Robbie ahead of me, the beast behind me letting out a roar as it saw me. I slammed the door shut and we sped along the short corridor until we came to another door. As I opened it, the zombie burst through the door behind me, splintering the wood as it came through shoulder first, losing its balance and falling to the ground, its arms trying to push itself back up even as it slid along the tiled floor. I pulled the door open and ran into a large storage room.

There was nowhere for us to hide. I quickly searched for something that could be used as a weapon but there was nothing and then foot falls closed in on the door. I pushed Robbie into the far corner and stood in front of him, protectively. He crouched behind me and his sobs finally overtook him. The door shattered as the creature burst through with a howl, landing in a sprinter's starting position, its head down. I raised my fists, the only thing I had left to defend the boy with. I hoped that when this thing stood up that it was not as big as the prisoner beast from Usk. From behind me, Robbie's voice had become a high pitched whine.

'Oh no, oh no, oh no…'

As brave as I was trying to be, I could not stop my knees from trembling.

The zombie began to rise. It only had one shoe, the other foot was clad in a blood stained white sock. It had left a trail of blood behind it. Its jeans were clean. Whatever it had been wearing on top had once been a colour other than red, but now it was a deep scarlet. It was matted and clung to the zombie's body. Its eyes were completely white. A massive tear ran across its neck and it continued to bleed from its left ear.

'Nick?' I asked, my heart finally breaking, my head finally believing that this was going to be the end, and that I was not going to be able to save Robbie, just like I had been unable to save his sisters, his father, or my brother.

The monster hissed at me, bearing its teeth, raising its hands like some low budget Dracula. If Robbie hadn't been right behind me, I would have stepped backwards.

Instead I did the only thing I had left.

'Nick, don't do this', I pleaded.

He hissed again, leapt forward, closing the gap between us to less than two metres. My breath was pumping in and out through my nose, tears were building in my eyes.

'Nick?'

He opened his mouth to snarl again. His teeth snapped together. And then he turned his head to the side, lowering the gaze of its dead eyes from my face and down towards my legs. I felt a tug at the back of my jogging trousers and looked down. Robbie was peering around me, looking at the beast that had once been his father. Nick snapped his jaw together again and Robbie recoiled for an instant. He lent forward again.

'Dad?'

Nick snarled, but it held less fury. It was almost a question.

'Nick…' I began but I didn't know how to continue. I was terrified. Robbie was terrified.

Nick took a step backwards and then he made that noise we had heard for so long from outside our gate.

'MMMMMMMMMMMMMMMM', he groaned

'Daddy, Daddy', pleaded Robbie, still hiding behind me.

Nick looked down at the boy and then up at me.

'MMMMMMMMMMMMMMMM' he repeated.

'Matt, make him stop, make him…'

'MMMMMM', Nick moaned.

'ATE', he added.

'MMMMMM...ATE', he repeated, looking deep into my eyes.

He looked down at Robbie and then up at me once more.

'MMM...ATE', he said before he turned and walked away, leaving Robbie and I alone in the storeroom.

***

We waited for over half an hour. I had fallen to my knees and wrapped Robbie in my arms and we cried on each other's' shoulders until there were no more tears left to fall. We didn't talk, we didn't mention his father or his sisters but we knew who we were crying for.

'I think we should go now', I whispered and Robbie nodded. I touched my nose. Although it had stopped bleeding it now held a crack halfway along.

If I survived this then I was going to have a very noticeable souvenir.

I decided that the thought of dying in this room, hiding like rats, was more frightening than facing whatever was outside.

We edged through each door and out from behind the bar. I gestured that Robbie should wait while I snuck outside to ensure the way was clear. I stepped over the cleaner's body, looked left, in the direction we would have to run. The mashed up Range Rover and police car remained in place. The horn continued to blare. Steam rose from both bonnets. All along the road and the pavement, streaks of blood and gore lay as memorials to the end of humanity. There was, however, none of the infected to be seen. I turned my head to the right and felt the breath suck out of my body.

Hundreds of zombies lined the road. They were all looking directly at me. I could see their shoulders rise and fall as they breathed. They looked like they were ready to start a marathon, but

I knew it would only be a sprint and then they would fall on Robbie and I, feasting on our flesh or turning us into one of their own.

And then Nick stepped to the front of the horde. He raised one hand to them and lifted his chin towards me. With a motion of his head he was telling me to go.

I reached back inside and grasped Robbie by the hand, leading him around the dead body on the floor and out into the street. I made sure he did not look to the right but as we turned left towards the stadium, I took a moment to glance back. Nick continued to hold his arm up, stopping the infected attacking us. Two smaller zombies ran out from the crowd and stood either side of him. As I stepped out of sight I was sure I saw him reach down and take their hands in his.

We approached the entrance to the stadium. The sniper was still in place and he pivoted his rifle towards us. I raised my arms and showed them my hands. Robbie copied me.

'We're human', I shouted and we began to walk forward towards the manhole cover.

'We're human', I shouted again and then there were more faces at the window and the rifle had been placed aside. I was sure I heard someone say 'he's back.'

I knelt down and lifted the metal cover. I took Robbie's hand and guided him into position so he could safely make his way down the ladder. He looked past me, back the way he came.

'Dad?' he said.

I looked over my shoulder and saw Nick, alone, standing watching us.

'No', I said, choosing to misunderstand Robbie's word. 'But I hope I'll do for now.'

More from E-Volve Books

Zombies II: Inhuman
Eric S. Brown

What if in a world where the dead walk and the human race faces extinction evolution were to step in and bless a special few with powers far beyond normal man. Could someone who can run as fast as the speed of light or someone who can control energy and channel it through her body truly make a difference at the end of time? Does telepathy work on zombies? Would these powerful few seek to save the world or rule it and how would we normal humans feel about them? Will these super-beings be wiped out by the zombie hordes or save the human race? Plus tales of zombies in space, zombies in the old west, and some very hungry zombie animals-this one has it all.

Dead Girl's Blog
Donna Burgess

Meet Audrey Scott. She has it all. She's the
most popular girl at Lincoln High and dates Tommy
Barker, the cutest boy in the senior class. She has a
credit card with no limit, is head cheerleader and
was probably going to be homecoming queen again
this year—until she was bitten by a Deader. Worst
part of it? He ruined her best jeans.

But that's just the tip of the putrid iceberg. Now,
Audrey is beginning to fester. She doesn't smell
very fresh. Her hair comes out, along with pieces of
scalp. Her friends no longer want to hang out with
her. Tommy has moved on to a new girl.

And poor Audrey is suddenly wearing Depends
and hanging with her lame younger sister, Cindy.

The world isn't like it was. Disease is in the air
and people have become infected. The dead are no
longer buried because they won't stay put in their
graves. They are sent out to big, green pastures with

electric fences, where they remain until they rot away to nothing.

Told in blog form, this short is an introduction to Notes from the End of the World, a dark young adult novel by Donna Burgess, scheduled for release in 2012

2558881R00187

Printed in Great Britain
by Amazon.co.uk, Ltd.,
Marston Gate.